Acknowledgements

First I would like to thank my husband. For dealing with a messy house, for cooking dinner when I was busy at the keyboard, and for believing in me, for pushing me to publish. I love you.

Thank you, Nina, for always standing behind me, beside me, pushing me to be a better writer. You always called me on the messy writing, and made me a better writer because of it. You are my bestie, and will always be. Love ya girl!

To Christi and Cheryl, for letting me bounce ideas off of you and for motivating me when the last thing I wanted to do was put this dream on paper. You guys rock!

To my street team members: Jennifer, Autumn, Cheryl, Christi, Isis, and Johnnie-Marie. Y'all promoted my books and supported me through all of this.

Chapter One

Addie

Addie took one look at the parking lot of the bar and grinned. It was packed, had to be packed, with hot men and lots of alcohol. Just what she and her friends, Gemma and Autumn, wanted. After the first week of school, all teaching kids younger than eight, they needed the escape of dancing and sweaty men. They had to travel two hours just to get to a decent bar near the city, but they all thought it was worth it.

"Are we going in or are you just going to stare at the bar in excitement?" Autumn tossed her bold, copper colored hair behind her bare shoulder. Her one shoulder top and short black shorts were going to knock the guys dead.

Gemma, whose Asian heritage stood out with the shape of her face and the silkiness of her dark hair, wore a strapless turquoise dress and added a few inches to her height with her nude heels. "I need to get in there and get a drink. I need to relax."

Addie laughed. "Then let's go in." She'd waited all week for this release. She wanted to dance, drink, and have a good time with her friends and maybe pick up a cute guy to go home with.

The bouncer didn't card them and waved them through. He was familiar with the girls since they came by a lot during the school year. Music pumped loud as they passed through the doorway. People stood in the hallway that led to the club area, and the girls squeezed through to get past.

Addie was glad she'd decided against wearing a dress and instead settled on dark skinny jeans, black stilettos, and a royal purple spaghetti strapped shirt that showed off her tan from the summer. She didn't want to have to worry about some pervy guy sticking his hand up her dress and her having to break his face. At least in this, all she'd have to worry about would be someone grabbing her ass.

All week she'd looked forward to this outing. Her third graders hadn't gotten used to the structure of the school year yet and seriously pushed their limits. Especially after Labor Day weekend. She'd thought maybe they'd wear themselves out, but no. Not one of them could sit still this week, like they'd gotten high on gallons of sugar.

The air inside the club was thick and heavy from the

bodies on the dance floor. Once inside the dance room, Autumn pulled them to the left and snagged a tall table near the large mirrored walls.

"I don't want to fight anyone for a table, we need to claim it now." She fanned her face and chest. "There are so many people. It's about a thousand degrees in here."

Gemma shook her head and smiled. "There's about that many people here. Hopefully some of them will be extremely sexy men."

Addie scanned the packed room. The dance floor on the first level was full. She let her gaze travel over the dancers to the second floor where there was a bar, games, and food. It looked less packed. "Let's go to the second floor. We might be able to breathe, and I could use that drink we talked about."

"That's a good idea." Autumn led them back through the throngs of people to the left side staircase.

Addie followed her friends, the music vibrating through her body. She caught a few men staring, and why wouldn't they? She tossed her black waves over her shoulder and sent them coy smiles. Maybe tonight she wouldn't have to pay for her drinks.

"Ooh, look! Three seats at the bar!" Autumn nearly shoved some girls out of the way before they could claim the seats first.

Addie tried to hide her laughter at their bitchy looks as she slid onto the middle stool. She thought about something fruity to drink and frowned.

The very hot bartender stopped in front of her and shot her a cocky grin. "What can I get you?"

Addie eyes roamed over his fitted black t-shirt before meeting his gaze. She knew guys loved the dark blue of her eyes and that the dark color of her hair made them stand out more, especially when she lined them with gray liner. Her lips tilted just a bit on the right side, showing a dimple. "I want a shot of Fireball whiskey."

The bartender's eyebrows rose and Addie heard her friends trying to hide their snickers. "That's a big girl drink. Think you can handle it?"

Addie tilted her head to the side, a cascade of hair falling to her chest. His eyes traveled lower before they shot back to her face. "I can handle a lot of things."

"Oh God." Autumn let out the laugh she was trying to hide. "Just stop. Take him to the back room if you're going to, but don't torture us this way."

"For real." Gemma smiled. "I'll have a rum and Coke."

"I'll take an Absolut Stress." Autumn fanned herself again and looked over her shoulder at a group of guys playing pool in the corner. She nudged Gemma and nodded in that direction.

Gemma's chocolate colored eyes widened and then narrowed on the dark skinned man with a sleeve of tribal tattoos on his left arm. "Dibs. He's mine."

Addie winked at the bartender before tossing back her shot. The strong taste of Red Hots burned its way down her throat, and she loved the heat in her stomach. She tapped the shot glass on the counter, her signal for another one. The bartender grinned and poured another. She knocked it back and turned on the stool to see what the girls were talking about.

Each muscled, each tattooed, each someone Addie might want to mess around with for a night or two. She slid off the stool, sent a wink over her shoulder to the bartender, and followed Gemma and Autumn to the pool table. The dark skinned man looked up from where he lined up a shot with the cue and immediately saw Gemma.

Gemma shot him a brilliant smile, one Addie knew few men could resist, and waved her fingers. The guy grinned, showing a row of white teeth, and turned his attention back to the cue. He took the shot, hitting the eight ball in, and the guys around him groaned.

"Damn it, Carter. I thought you said you'd take it easy

on me." A blonde guy shook his head and pulled out his wallet. He slapped a twenty on the edge of the table with a playful scowl.

The dark skinned guy grinned at him, slid the twenty into his back pocket. "I couldn't lose in front of such beautiful ladies."

The other guys' heads turned to look at Addie, Gemma, and Autumn. Carter walked around the table to Gemma and when his eyes ran over her and his gaze met hers, Addie saw the spark there. Guys always fell hard for Gemma. She was a catch.

Autumn winked at the blonde. "Wanna play again?" She ran a finger down the cue Carter left on the table.

"Sure. What's the bet?" He asked.

He had no idea what he was getting into. Autumn was a shark when it came to the game and wouldn't lose unless she wanted to. "You buy me and my friends' drinks tonight."

"Deal." He grinned and Addie could see the satisfaction on his face already. "And if I win, you dance with me. All night."

Addie smirked at the undertone of the bet. Autumn was going to eat him alive.

"Deal." Autumn licked her lips while he set up the

balls.

"Get her, Caleb," Carter whooped from beside Gemma.

Addie shook her head, smiling. Tonight was definitely going to be fun. She just needed to decide which one she wanted. Carter and Caleb seemed to be claimed already and she wasn't the kind of girl to step in on her friend's territories. One guy stood to the right of the table, redheaded but silent. She decided against him, he wasn't paying attention to her. Two other guys stood near a dark corner, arms crossed. They both wore identical grins on their faces, twins down to the matching firefighter t-shirts they wore.

That would explain the amount of muscle and camaraderie. Addie sidled over, smiled at them. "Hey, boys. Mind if I stand over here with you?"

"Not at all," the one on the left said.

"Want a stool?" the other one turned to the darkened corner. "Finn, be a gentleman and give the beautiful lady your seat."

"Fine." The husky voice spoke from the darkness.

Addie's body snapped to attention and her lips parted. That voice brushed over her nerve endings and lit a fire in her blood. She leaned toward the darkness to glimpse the owner.

10

The stool came out first in a pair of strong hands. Her eyes traveled up the tattooed arms, almost gasping at the muscles, to the short sleeves of his navy t-shirt. When he emerged fully, she resisted the urge to bite her lip, a free invitation to guys like him.

He had a short cut of blonde hair and intense green eyes that reminded her of the Northern Lights that her students were studying. The eyes weren't as welcoming, and in that instant she saw an ocean of pain before he blinked it away and scowled at her.

That brought her attention to his full lips. Lips that would've made him look almost girlish if not for the craggy lines of his face and short beard stubble.

"Here." He held out the stool. "I'm going to get a drink."

He brushed past her and she inhaled the spicy scent he wore. She took a deep breath, tried to calm the shock of emotions he'd woken in her from that one glance. He looked like trouble, more than she wanted to get into. Something that would be much more than a few nights of fun. She shook it off, looked to the twins that stood on either side of her.

"Let's start our own bet, boys." She shot them a mischievous grin.

Chapter Two

Finn

What the hell just happened? He'd taken one look at those deep blue eyes, eyes that reminded him of the lakes at home, and he'd tripped. The hard shell that he'd built around himself had taken a hit and he'd had to fight hard just to keep it in place. Sweat beaded on his forehead and he wiped it off with his forearm. He wasn't sure why the girl shook him that way, but he intended to stay far away from her.

The demons he fought so hard to contain scratched at him, raw and hungry. He curled his hands into fists as he approached the bar. He couldn't leave since he'd promised the guys he'd stay out tonight. It was the first night he'd been out of the fire station to do something other than work since he'd been back. He couldn't break his word.

"Something hard and strong." He told the bartender. While he waited he turned around, resting his elbows on the bar behind him, and risked a glance back at the table. The girl tossed her dark hair over her shoulder and laughed at something Nate and Noah said to her. Probably regaling her with tales of their bravery. Aaron stood silent, watching the pool game. The redhead usually stayed quiet until he had something to say. People didn't normally notice him until he did.

Finn's attention was pulled back to the girl, something he couldn't fight at the moment. His abdomen clenched at a look of her lips and he grit his teeth. He hadn't experienced any desire for sex since he returned to the States. Why the hell was this girl waking that up now?

He didn't have time for this, didn't deserve it.

"Hey. Your drink's ready." The bartender slid the drink over to him.

The hot sting of alcohol hit Finn's nose as he took a big sip. To lose himself in this, to drown his memories in the amber liquid, would be too easy. He slid the bartender a ten and motioned for him to keep the change. The bartender's eyes weren't on him, though. It was on the dark haired vixen. The quick slice of possessiveness that shot through him shocked Finn so much he almost decided to break his word and run to the station. Run far away from the hot little piece of trouble that beckoned him.

Instead, he took his time walking back to the guys. He was never one to drag his feet, wanting to take problems head on, but he had a feeling that if he took this particular one on, he wouldn't survive it. He glanced over her again, staring first at the tight ass jeans and then the purple top that fell at just the right way to show off the swell of her breasts, which caused a swell in his pants. He took another swig and tore his gaze away from her. He focused on the pool table, on the game going between Caleb and the female redhead. Standing by Nathan so he wouldn't watch the girl on the stool, he forced himself to stay focused on the game.

The redhead was working Caleb. From the satisfied smirk on her ivory face, he could tell she waited to take him down at the knees. That girl knew what she was doing even if Caleb was too lust-bitten to realize it.

The dark haired vixen laughed and his abdomen clenched again. Jesus, the husky sound tore right through him. He wanted to push the twins out of the way and crash his mouth to hers. Nothing gentle. Primal need rose in his blood and he fought hard to quell it. He was so used to being bored around women that he almost lost his self-control and took action.

"Win that bet, Autumn!" She clapped her hands and

laughed again.

His grip tightened around the glass.

"Come on, girl!" The Asian girl called and leaned closer to Carter as he whispered something in her ear.

Would Carter take the girl home? He'd sworn off women after a bad break up several months ago and this girl was the first to catch Carter's eye in a while. Finn wanted his friend to be happy, and if this girl did it, he'd love her for it.

"Gemma, quit flirting and get out of my way." Autumn winked over her shoulder at her friend as she aimed for the eight ball.

Caleb seemed to hold his breath while he watched her take the shot.

She hit it, sinking it in the right corner pocket.

"Damn." Caleb grinned. "Marry me."

Autumn smiled and tilted her head to the side. "Take the drink orders and we'll talk about it. Addie, what do you want?"

Addie. Such a simple name for an explosive woman. It fit her in an odd sort of way. He'd expected something exotic like Catalina, but the traditional name whispered through his mind.

"Another Fireball whiskey."

That fit also, since the husky tone of her voice reminded him of the heat of whiskey burning through him. He wasn't surprised she didn't want one of those fruity things girls usually drink. She was wild enough to want the harder stuff.

"Damn girl, okay." Caleb chuckled and turned to Gemma. "What can I get for you?"

"I'll have a rum and Coke please." Gemma laid a hand on Carter's arm. "But first I want to dance."

"Sure thing." Carter steered her toward the stairs.

Finn watched them walk off and could practically see the sparks crackling between the two of them, even from a distance. He held the drink in his hand, not wanting to rely on it any more than he needed to. He'd seen to many of his fellow soldiers succumb to the numbness that alcohol gave them.

"Our turn." Nathan slapped Noah on the back. "Whoever loses has to drive Mom to see Grandpa next weekend."

"Deal." Noah started to rack the balls.

The air electrified around him as he realized no one stood between him and Addie now. He kept himself still, thinking maybe she wouldn't try to engage him in conversation if he did.

"So, what's with the rudeness?" Her voice drifted to him.

Damn it. He answered before he thought about it. "It's nothing."

Her eyebrows rose. "Oh, nothing. Awesome. I always turn into a giant asshole when nothing's going on."

He looked at her, wanted to snap at her, until he saw the humor shining in those deep blue eyes.

"There's a teensy weensy grin on your face. Careful, people may see it." She grinned at him and her face lit up. "That's not so hard, is it?"

The muscles around his mouth actually hurt and he wondered how long it'd been since he'd really smiled. Not fake smiled, not pretended to make someone else happy. A second later he saw they were almost touching. Somehow he'd moved closer to her without noticing.

"What do the tattoos mean on your arms?"

His amusement evaporated. Absently he brushed his fingertips over a part of his left forearm sleeve.

"What is that?" She asked softly, the only reason he answered.

"It's a shield with the Celtic warrior knot on it." Finn battled the grief back, told himself that he wouldn't show weakness in front of anyone. He started when she laid a hand on his arm.

She quickly withdrew her hand. "Sorry. I didn't mean to freak you out."

To keep the grief at bay, he turned back into that asshole. "Maybe you shouldn't touch people without their permission."

Fire ignited in her eyes. "Maybe you shouldn't be such an asshole." She snapped back. "Maybe you should realize that not every woman wants to jump your bones, damn it."

"Looks like someone's pissed that a guy turned her down." His voice lowered a few degrees. He told himself he didn't care about the hurt that flashed in her gaze. That it didn't matter that he was being a bastard. He couldn't let anyone close.

She pushed on his chest. "That would hurt my feelings, you know, if I wanted to get in your pants. Which I don't. Because you're a complete bastard."

His mouth twisted. She was going for blood, a warrior at heart. He admired her even as she irritated the hell out of him. Out of the corner of his eye he saw that the twins had stopped their game and stared at them. Finn grit his teeth, feeling his self-control splinter a little. He didn't care how much he might admire her, he had to walk away. Now. Without looking back at her or the twins, he headed to the stairs. Maybe if he went outside, got some fresh air, he'd regain control.

Chapter Three

Addie

Addie hated Mondays. Mondays were the devil's balls, especially after the weekend she had. None of the guys at the bar had caught her eye, so she'd spent the weekend alone. After that idiot had argued with her, she hadn't wanted to spend it with any man.

That was a lie. Addie was brutally honest, even with herself, so she leaned back in the chair behind her desk and sighed. She'd wanted to spend it with him. He'd lit a fire in her that she knew could get out of control but she wanted it anyway, which was stupid. He was hot, and broody, and had all those tight muscles and tattoos.

He'd also had scars. Not physically that she could see, but when she'd mentioned the tattoos, she'd seen the shadow fall over his face. All she'd wanted to do was comfort him, which was weird for her, and he'd freaked the hell out. What a bastard.

"What are you sulking about?" Gemma walked into the classroom, clothes much more conservative than Friday night. "I know you hate Mondays, which is why I brought you this."

"Bless you." Addie took the proffered coffee cup and took a sip. "Thanks."

Gemma settled on the corner of Addie's desk. "You're still thinking of that guy from the bar, aren't you? He got under your skin."

Addie frowned, picked at the rim of her cup. Her nail polish was chipped, which meant she needed to redo them soon. The principal wanted everyone to stay 'professional'. "I don't understand what his problem was."

"Carter said he's been like this every since he moved here." Gemma laughed when Addie's eyes widened.

Addie smiled at her friend, not willing to cave. "You spent all weekend with Carter, didn't you? You like him."

Gemma's answering smile lit her eyes. "I did and I do. You know I never stay all weekend, but there's something about him. He's sexy and sweet, which is a hell of a combination."

"I missed out this weekend." Addie set the cup down, shrugged. "It's okay, though, I can handle the loss. Have you seen Autumn yet?" Autumn usually beat them to school.

"She texted me a few minutes ago, said she's driving from Caleb's place." Gemma tapped Addie's phone. "Did you turn the sound back on?"

"No." Addie sighed. She always forgot to turn the sound back on, and usually missed a lot of important information that way. She picked up her phone, realized she had messages from both her sisters, Autumn and Gemma. After reading and answering, she set it back down. "I'm going to dinner at mom's tonight."

"I'm seeing Carter again. We talked about setting up a field trip for the third graders to go see the firehouse. Did you know they're Sanctuary Bay firefighters?"

Addie didn't and couldn't quell her excitement that Finn lived in her town. "You said Carter told you that he moved here?"

A mischievous glint twinkled in Gemma's dark eyes. "If you want all this info on Finn, you should ask him yourself." She laughed at Addie's face as she slid off the desk. "I've got to get my classroom ready. We're starting to learn about the Civil War and I have to set up the visual aids I made."

"Good luck. We're doing comprehension and grammar."

Gemma waved as she left.

Addie's mouth twisted. On one hand she was excited to see Finn again on the field trip, especially if he was in his firefighter uniform. On the other, she was terrified of it. Just from that one night she couldn't get him out of her mind and she knew she stood on a slippery slope. She didn't want to fall.

§ §

She walked into her parents' house that evening and immediately the stress melted from her body. There was something about hearing her family's laughter that brought a smile to her face no matter happened in her life. The scent of pot roast and potatoes reached her and her stomach growled. She didn't cook, didn't like to, so she only ate home-cooked meals when her mom made them.

Helena and Lucia, her twin nieces, looked up when she entered. Lucia squealed, jumping up and down, and launched herself at Addie. Addie laughed and caught her, wrapping her in a hug. Lucia's light perfume tickled her nose and Addie's heart ached. Her sweet nieces were honest-to-God teenagers now. She could only imagine how Victoria felt.

"Hey, Addie." Helena smiled and waved from where she stood, the Wii remote swinging from her wrist. "I passed the science test. I'll be in the advanced class next semester."

"That's awesome!" Addie grinned and high-fived Helena. She tried not to be obvious as she checked her over, making sure that she was still okay with her mom dating again. Addie knew that any day now Nick would move in, but both her sister and he wanted to make sure the girls were well adjusted before that happened.

In the beginning Helena hated Nick because of her douche-bag father, but after the wreck she was in, and her father didn't even bother to visit her in the hospital, Helena's eyes opened. She clearly saw Nick was a great guy now.

"I know, I can't wait." Helena's eyebrow lifted. "Are you ready for some bowling?"

"In just a minute." Addie tugged gently on the end of Helena's pony-tail. "I'm going to go say hi to everyone first."

"Okay." Helena turned her attention back to the TV and started a game with her sister.

Addie decided that the color in Helena's cheeks and the brightness of her eyes told her what she needed to know.

She'd adjusted to her mom and Nick's relationship. When Addie entered the kitchen her mom was at the sink, washing the dishes she'd used during cooking. Victoria's boyfriend, Nick, stood beside her, drying the dishes when Cecelia finished rinsing.

Victoria and Halle sat at the bar chopping vegetables for the salad. Her mother usually had salads for a side, but made them with a variety so no one tired of them.

"Get your butt over here and help." Victoria waved her little knife to the stool between her and Halle.

Addie grinned and went to help. Halle smiled at her and Addie worried because the smiles weren't nearly as bright as they used to be. For that alone she wanted to junk punch Halle's cheating ex husband. She'd gotten the satisfaction of hitting him in the face the night Halle found out about his dirty ways but sometimes wished for more. To help with dinner, she sat on the stool and started chopping red and yellow bell peppers.

"How's work, Halle?" She watched her fingers as she worked.

"Good, working in a hospital is hard but rewarding. I love the patients." Halle tucked a piece of her short, dark bob behind her ear. "It took a little while to get used to it, but I love it."

Addie nudged her. "I knew you'd like it."

Halle rolled her eyes. "Because you're *always* right."

"Yep." Addie laughed at her. "And how's the business, Vic?" She watched her sister tear her eyes from Nick's ass as he helped their mom. She couldn't blame her, Nick was a hottie.

Victoria blushed when she saw Addie watching her. "It's going great. A lot more clients have signed up for work now that tourist season has dwindled down."

"Helena looks great. Have you heard from Roger?" Addie wanted to junk punch the girls' father, too. And Finn. Maybe she should start a list.

Victoria shook her head. "No, the damn bastard has completely fallen off the radar. Which is fine with me. They have Nick."

"Yeah they do." Nick called over his shoulder. Cecelia giggled.

Addie arched a brow at Victoria, who shook her head in amusement. She wanted desperately to tell her sisters about Finn, but that would have to wait. If she said anything about a man around her mother, her mom would have the wedding planned and grandkids' names picked out. She didn't want that kind of pressure on her. Her mother hated the fact that she'd decided to be a bachelorette for life.

When dinner was ready, they went into the dining room, each putting their cell phones into a basket on a side table. Addie's fingers twitched, she felt lost without her phone in her hand, but rules were rules.

Her dad sat at the head of the table and said grace. When he finished, he smiled at his family.

If she could find a man like her dad, one that had that strength and conviction and absolute love for his wife and family, she'd maybe think about giving up her bachelorette status, but so far she'd only met total douchebags. Conversations immediately started around her and she was content with listening to her family's laughter and voices.

"Mom, can I have a cell phone?" Lucia asked as soon as it got quiet.

Victoria's mouth dropped. "Really? You want one already?"

"I'm like the only one without a phone. The girls on the cheer squad keep asking when I'm going to get one." Lucia batted her eyelashes.

Victoria turned to Nick, eyes wide. Addie would've giggled at how shell-shocked she was, but didn't think it'd go over well.

"We'll talk it over and let you know," Victoria told her. When Lucia squealed, Victoria held up a hand. "That doesn't mean our answer is going to be yes."

Lucia didn't seem to care, her face brightened.

"You know, we didn't have phones when I was little and we did just fine," Wes, their grandfather, told them.

"Yeah, but that was like, years ago."

Addie tried to hold her laugh in and choked on her food. Halle patted her back until Addie could swallow, trying to hold back her own laughter. It was good to see her sister laughing. Trevor was lucky she didn't own a gun or his cheating ass would be dead.

Later that evening, when she entered her apartment, she shed her work clothes in favor of yoga pants and a comfy t-shirt. She pulled her mass of black hair up in a messy ponytail and removed her make-up, then sat on the couch to watch DVR.

She was lonely. It wasn't normal, because she loved being alone. When all her sorority sisters wanted to get a place after college, she'd turned them down. She'd had enough of living with several women. Talk about drama.

This loneliness was probably because she'd witnessed the solidarity between Nick and Victoria. Her sister went through enough with her ex-husband and Addie was happy she was happy. That didn't mean it would be a good fit for her. Independence suited her more.

Maybe she should get a pet. A kitten would be cute, because she wouldn't really be home enough for a dog. She'd think about getting one.

The next morning at school, Autumn waited for her in her classroom.

"Hey, girl. You really need to turn your sound back on." Autumn stood from where she sat in Addie's chair.

"Damn it." Addie reached into her purse, turned the sound back up. "What's up?"

"Carter and Caleb invited us to the sports bar tonight. I think Finn's going to be there." Autumn waggled her eyebrows at Addie suggestively.

"I don't know. He's too...intense. And a bastard. Why would I want to spend more time with him?"

Autumn lifted a shoulder, let it fall. "You don't have to spend time with him. The twins were interested in you, and besides, you can show Finn what he's missing from your sexy ass."

Gemma shot into the classroom. "Did you tell her about tonight?"

"She doesn't want to go," Autumn said.

Gemma set her purse down on the edge of Addie's desk. "That's a load of bull. You know you want to see him again."

"I hate it when you gang up on me." Addie sighed. "Fine, I'll go. But only because you want me to."

"You know that's not the only reason."

Addie also hated when her friends were right.

Chapter Four

Finn

He had no idea how he'd let the guys talk him into coming to this bar, knowing Addie would be here. For some reason he couldn't stop himself from wanting to see her again, even if she had a caustic attitude. After a quick glance around the bar, he saw his friends sitting in a booth near the back, facing one of the flat screen TV's hanging on the wall. He saw Addie sitting there, laughing at something Caleb said.

Steeling himself, he crossed the bar, weaving through the tables until he reached the booth.

"Hey man, I thought you were going to stand us up." Caleb slid closer to Autumn, making room across from Addie.

"Had to finish some things at the firehouse." Finn lowered himself to the booth, thankful his back was to the wall and he could watch the people around him. He couldn't have people sneaking up, bringing on some of his memories of war. Addie's laugh quieted as he sat, and he flicked a glance her way. She wore shorts and a t-shirt with her hair in a pony-tail. He preferred how she looked now to Friday night.

"Finn's a workaholic." Carter slid him a menu across the table. "He stays at the firehouse 24-7."

"All work and no play." Addie tilted her head and he watched the curve of her neck. He felt himself harden and curled his fist on his thigh. "Do you not want to have any fun?"

He heard the suggestion in her voice, decided to ignore it. "No."

Her eyes narrowed, but she didn't say anything else.

"Jesus, Finn. What's gotten into you?" Nate shook his head.

"Nothing." Finn picked up the menu, pretended to read the words on it. He couldn't focus, though, not with Addie sitting across from him. Or with the pressure that closed in on his chest. Too many people crowded the bar and his eyes darted through the crowd.

An awkward silence followed until Addie spoke up. "It's okay, he's not bothering me. So, have you guys had any interesting calls lately?"

Just like that, the tension in the air dissipated. Finn peeked over his menu at her, but couldn't figure out if she did that for him, or if she couldn't care less what he felt. The pressure in his chest eased as he looked at her.

"We had to rescue a cat from the top of a sailboat this morning. The owner was afraid of heights and I didn't see her climbing up there to get him," Noah told her. The girls "awwed" at the same time and Finn forced himself not to roll his eyes.

"I thought fire departments didn't do stuff like that."

"In a town this small, we don't really tell the citizens no," Carter told Autumn.

"I want a kitten." Addie twirled the straw in her drink. "I was thinking about visiting the shelter and seeing if they had any."

"Really? You think you can take care of it?" Gemma winked at her friend.

He wondered if Addie would take offense but she threw her head back and laughed a husky laugh that twisted his insides.

"Yes, it's not like a puppy. They're pretty much litter trained when you get them, aren't they?" Addie's deep blue eyes twinkled and he resisted the urge to smile.

"They're cute," Autumn told her. "I'll go with you when

you want to pick one out."

"Okay."

"We've set up the field trip for next Friday, so the kids have time to get the forms filled out by their parents," Gemma said. "You boys better put on a good show."

"We plan on it." Carter kissed the back of her hand before setting their intertwined hands on the table.

Finn watched Addie's face, trying to read the reaction she had to Gemma and Carter. He couldn't figure out what she felt about it and wasn't sure he really wanted to. She seemed like a wild character, one that reminded him of one of his sisters, and he didn't want to get wrapped up in something like that.

They ordered their food and he liked that she ordered nachos, which was one of his favorites. She even ordered extra jalapeños. A girl after his own heart.

Throughout the meal he stayed silent, but observed his friends and especially Addie. The girl was a fireball of energy and laughter. She enjoyed life to the fullest and spread her joy to the people she was around, affecting even him. The muscles in his face stretched and he decided this girl was dangerous to his resolve.

She shot him a few glances, and his pulse rocketed each time. Yeah, this girl was definitely dangerous.

When the night was over, he squashed any temptation to follow her to her car and push her against it. After watching her all night he had one thing on his mind. He wanted to feel her lips against his, her hands in his hair, pulling him closer. He had no doubt she'd be a wildcat in bed.

Instead he walked off without saying good-bye and headed to the only gym in town. He needed to burn all this extra energy swirling inside and he wasn't going to do it by having sex with whoever was around. He'd just see Addie's face anyway.

His phone rang. "Hello?"

The caller didn't say anything. In the background he heard muted conversations.

"Hello? Anyone there?"

Nothing but the talking in the background. A frisson of unease slid down his spine and then the dial tone rang in his ear. His mouth twisted and he put the phone back down. Told himself to relax, someone just had the wrong number.

The gym was nearly empty this late. He headed to the lockers and changed into a pair of sweats and a t-shirt, then taped his knuckles and went to the punching bags. He was the only one on them, so he relaxed a little.

For an hour he beat on the punching bag with jabs,

kicks, and solid hits. When she'd creep into his mind again, he'd force her out with a harder punch. He didn't need to get involved, not after Mia. He was over wild girls.

God, and as he thought of Mia, the other stuff exploded into his mind. The gunfire, the blood, the shouts of his friends. His chest heaved as he stopped fighting the punching bag. Glancing down at the Celtic warrior shield on his arm, he traced it with his fingers. He and Isaac had gotten it before they'd deployed to Afghanistan, solidifying their lifetime friendship.

Someone cleared their throat behind him. He spun around, but relaxed when he saw the owner, Luke, standing a few feet away. The guy held out a chilled bottle of water.

"You look like you need this." Luke continued to hold out the bottle. "In fact, you look like you could use something stronger."

Finn struggled to get his breathing under control. He didn't want anyone to see how much he hurt or how close he was to losing that control he so desperately needed. "Thanks." He grasped the bottle but didn't drink it.

Luke watched him closely. "You're new around here."

Finn nodded.

"You're on the fire department?" Luke sauntered closer, gestured to the water bottle. "People normally drink those."

Finn glanced at the bottle, gave in, and sipped.

"I'm having a get together at my house next Saturday for the football game. I'd like for you to come. It'll be a few close friends and family." Luke's lips lifted into a grin. "You look like you could use some distracting fun."

He almost refused, but Luke looked hopeful and he really didn't feel comfortable turning him down. The guy didn't seem like he'd take no for an answer. He could go for a while. "Sure."

"Great. I'll tell my brother you're coming. My nieces will be there, so we won't be getting too rowdy."

Finn nodded again.

"I'll leave you to it, then." Luke started to walk off.

"Thanks." Finn forced out. "For the water and for the invitation."

"Sure thing." Luke called back.

Finn stared at the water bottle in his hand, seeing it as more than a plastic container. It was a gesture of friendship, one Finn was uncomfortable with accepting. He'd go to the football party, be on his best behavior for the nieces, and leave as soon as he could.

On his way to the car after his gym session his text alert beeped. He checked the message, saw he was needed for a fire. He sped the entire way to the fire house and parked haphazardly. The guys were already there. He dashed to his gear and rushed to put it on. Adrenaline burst through his veins, enough to satisfy his craving of it from war, as he hung his air mask around his neck and shoved his feet into black boots.

"Come on, Finn." Nate passed him, getting into the driver's seat of the fire truck.

He hustled to join the others in the truck and sat behind Nate. Nate got the big truck moving, picking up speed. It didn't take them long to get to the outskirts of Sanctuary Bay. Flames and black smoke enveloped a beach house.

They hopped out of the truck, started on their duties. The police officer called to the scene walked up.

"No one home, neighbors said the fire started thirty minutes ago, but it's going up fast." He was a short, bald man with a muscular build. Finn knew him from some of the other calls.

The heat pushed on them as they connected the hose to the fire hydrant on the corner of the street. Finn was already sweating underneath his gear but he was used to the work, and loved the burn of his muscles as he fought the fire.

After fighting the fire for an hour, he looked up and realized that the neighbors crowded on the boardwalk across the street. They whispered among themselves and he resisted the urge to bark at them to move back. They weren't in harm's way where they stood, but they were too close for his liking. His chief, Dwayne, talked with the news crew from the city that had shown up.

The thought of his face being plastered all over the news made his skin crawl. He wanted to be done with this and get back to the station, out of the attention of several onlookers and the network.

"Finn, come look at this." Carter waved him to where the guys stood at the back of the fire truck.

Something meowed pitifully from a blanket that sat on the tailboard of the truck. Finn moved closer and saw a mass of gray fur poke its head out from under the thick, black blanket.

"We found her under the car. She's alone, no sign of any other kitten family." Caleb scratched the kitten under the chin with the tip of his index finger.

Finn's first thought was that Addie wanted a kitten. And here one sat, meowing pitifully at him like some fucking sign from God. Before he could think about it, he reached down and scooped the kitten up. "I know who wants this."

The guys stared at him. He dared them with a hard stare to say anything about what he was going to do with the kitten and who he was giving her to.

Chapter Five

Addie

Since the night of the sports bar, all she thought about was Finn. The way he looked and smelled. Why he acted like such an asshole and why she hadn't already written him off. Something about him got under her skin and she couldn't tell if she liked the sensation or not. So now, as she loaded up on the school bus with Gemma, Autumn, and their third grade classes, she decided not to worry about him. She'd decided that three times this morning but wasn't having any luck so far.

She sat with Autumn, while Gemma sat with one of the parents that was signed up as a chaperone. Kids' voices and giggles rose in the stuffy air of the bus as they left the school parking lot and headed toward the fire station. Addie knew this was coming and already swallowed some Excedrin. She didn't want to have a horrible headache when she saw Finn.

The hot sun beamed, making kids drop the bus windows with loud *thunks*.

"I think I'm going to break things off with Caleb." Autumn pulled her hair up in a messy bun.

"Not during the field trip, I hope." Addie used a brochure for the fire department to fan her face, then fanned the back of Autumn's neck. "I thought you were having fun with him."

Autumn shrugged. "I'm ready to move on."

"I wonder how he'll take that."

"His heart will be broken, naturally." Autumn glanced over at Gemma. "But I bet she and Carter will be long lasting."

Addie peered at her other friend, who was talked up a storm with the mom. She was so beautiful and sweet and Addie wanted what was best for her. If Carter was it, if she wanted to make that leap of faith, she'd support Gemma. "You really think so?"

Autumn nodded. "Don't question my relationship psychic powers. I'm never wrong. You and Finn will get together soon."

Addie laughed. "No."

Autumn raised a brow at her as they pulled into the fire station parking lot.

"Not unless he does something to change my mind." Addie turned and did another head count of her students. A few were absent today, and she wanted to make sure she left with the right amount of kids. Her pulse picked up and she was warm in places that had nothing to do with the heat outside. How did he affect her like this when she wasn't even sure she liked his attitude? Looks only took a person so far.

"Okay, kids." Gemma stood and it went quiet. "I want you to line up in the aisle, the front of the bus going first. We will show these fire fighters how mannerly we are. We will not run around like crazy kids full of red dye and sugar."

The kids quieted down like they always did when Gemma spoke. It had to have something to do with her calm demeanor. When they were in Addie's charge on field trips, they all mirrored her and acted a little wild. The seven moms that were chaperoning filed off first so they could get their groups together.

Addie glanced off the bus and saw the guys lined up in navy blue Sanctuary Bay fire fighter t-shirts and yellow firefighter pants with the red suspenders hanging loose. Her eyes immediately went to Finn and her breathing hitched. The sun's rays lit up the natural highlights in his blond hair and his green eyes looked more kind. Maybe it was because there were children around.

She came off the bus behind Gemma and Autumn and her back straightened. If he wasn't nice to these kids, or showed his asshole side, she'd make sure he hurt.

"Hey, kids." An older man stepped forward. "My name is Dwayne, and I'm the fire chief." He gestured to several of the men behind him. Addie struggled to keep her eyes on the chief. "This is my crew. Today we're going to show you what the fire station is like."

One of Addie's kids, a brown haired, talkative boy, raised his hand and Dwayne smiled at him.

"What's your name, son?"

"Tommy. Are we going to sit in the fire truck?" Tommy slid his hand down, grinned to show one of his front teeth missing. His mom smiled behind him and placed a hand on his shoulder.

"We sure are. First we'll show you the inside of the fire house, and you can slide down the poles." Dwayne chuckled when the kids cheered around them. "You can ask us any questions you have. Who's ready to get started?"

The kids cheered again.

"Let's go inside." Dwayne led them in through the giant garage where two fire trucks gleamed inside the bay.

"Do you have a puppy?" One of Gemma's girls asked.

"No, do you think we should get one?" Carter grinned at the girl and Gemma beamed at him.

Addie felt almost like she was intruding on an intimate moment between them, even if there were a bunch of people around. Emotions shone heavy in both of their eyes and she could see where Autumn got the idea they would last.

Finn fell into step beside her as they walked into the firehouse. Addie hated that she was aware of every movement he made, every glance that flicked her way. She didn't understand how she could be attracted to him when she couldn't stand him. It didn't make sense.

The kids squealed happily as they entered the station. The bottom floor was an open plan with rooms off to the sides. Firefighter gear hung on industrial size pegs near the door to the garage. A kitchen was off to the right with a large table that held at least fifteen chairs. In the middle of the room was a small living room which had a pool table and a large TV with a DVD player and game consoles. Addie wondered how often the firefighters actually had time to relax.

"Who cooks dinner? Does your mom come and do it?" Another little boy asked.

Chief Dwayne laughed. "Nope. We have to do all that on our own. Even our laundry. We also keep everything clean."

"That's no fun."

After a few minutes of letting the kids tour the bottom, Dwayne asked them if they wanted to go upstairs to the bunk room and slide down the poles.

Addie couldn't hold back her smile when the kids started to jump up and down. She, Autumn, and Gemma decided to stay down on the bottom floor to make sure no one got hurt.

The moms followed the twins and the chief up the stairs.

A little girl in Autumn's class, Abigail, turned to Finn and tugged on his bright yellow pants. "Is it scary going down the pole?"

Addie turned a little to see Finn's reaction.

He knelt down and looked the girl in the eyes. "The first time I went down I was a little scared, but it's fun. Like going down a slide. Do you like going down slides?"

Abigail nodded, her straight brown hair brushing her shoulders. "Will you go up there with me?"

"Sure." Finn's gaze moved to Addie and then back to the girl. He reached out a hand, and Abigail took it, her hand looking fragile in his.

Addie's heart squeezed at the sight. She had no idea why, and turned back to the poles so she could watch the kids slide down. Finn took the girl up the stairs, never letting go of her hand.

The kids started to slide down, laughing and shrieking. None fell, each having a death-grip on the silver pole. She heard the chief giving them advice, telling them not to put their legs so close around it so they slid down easier.

The kids' faces flushed and their eyes brightened. Each one wanted to go down again and ran back up the stairs.

"No running," Gemma called to them and they immediately slowed down.

"I wish they listened to me like that," Addie muttered.

"They don't because you're just as wild as they are." Autumn laughed at her.

Caleb, Carter, and Aaron stood by the poles, taking over the girls' duty of making sure no one fell.

"Do you really want to break it off with Caleb?" Addie asked when she caught Autumn watching his movements.

Autumn shrugged. "I think so. I'm not sure."

"Girls, we don't need to discuss this here." Gemma shot them a look.

Addie held up her hands. "Okay, okay."

When the kids finished sliding down the poles and exclaiming about the bunk room, the Chief gathered them up into a group. "Who wants to see the fire trucks now?"

The kids shrieked again. Addie noticed Finn watching her and raised a brow at him. What was his deal? Why did he want to be an ass and then stare at her in a way that caused her skin to catch fire? He looked away and walked ahead of them.

She couldn't help but watch the way he moved. She may think he was an ass, but he was a hot ass and she wasn't going to stop herself from looking.

The chief led them into the garage bay and stopped by the first fire truck. He placed a hand on it, a little reverently, and turned back to the kids. "How many of you have been on one of these?" None of the kids raised their hands. "We'll just have to fix that, won't we? Get in line outside both of the trucks and we'll show you around."

Addie helped herd the kids to the second fire truck, since Finn stood next to the chief. He confused her, a mix of emotions inside her, and she didn't want to deal with it right then.

Autumn stayed behind so she didn't have to deal with Caleb. Addie and Gemma walked to where Nate, Noah, Carter and Caleb started to show the kids the stuff on the truck. Addie watched Nate and Noah hold out one of the hoses to let the kids try and heft them up.

"Take some pictures." Gemma nudged Addie. "We can put them in the end of the year slideshow."

Addie pulled out her phone and started snapping pictures of the kids. Each had a perfect smile and looked like they were having the best time. Addie envied the easy way they lived, the easy way they saw everything around them with joy. When did that disappear for her? It's not like she'd had a hard childhood, far from it. Her parents and sisters were the best.

She shook off that mood and focused on taking pictures of the kids as they sat in the driver's seat or climbed in the back. They smiled goofily or stuck their tongues out when they noticed the phone in her hands. She loved these kids and a little of her heart broke each time students left her to go to fourth grade.

Carter helped them down as he talked to Gemma. She wondered what the topic of conversation was and if Gemma was really going to stick with him. Gemma deserved someone who would make her ridiculously happy.

After the kids played around for a while the Chief clapped his hands and they went back inside with their sack lunches to sit at the big table. Some of the kids sat on the couches or on the concrete floor.

Addie stood next to the counter with her little Lunchable. She loved the ham and cheese crackers and Capri Sun that came with it even though she knew it was made for kids. Autumn stood next to her while Gemma went and sat next to Carter on one of the couches.

"Oh my God, they're sharing their lunches. Where will it end?" Autumn rolled her eyes at the couple.

Addie couldn't help but laugh even if she was secretly jealous. "Leave them be. She's happy."

"Oh, I am. I'm just not ready to have all that mushy stuff shoved in my face." Autumn winked at Gemma when she saw them watching her.

"Can I talk to you for a minute?"

The rough voice washed over her before she turned and saw Finn standing a foot away.

"Go, talk." Autumn snatched the Lunchable away from Addie and shoved her toward him. "I'll keep an eye on the kids."

Addie narrowed her eyes at Autumn, but she didn't have an excuse now, so she followed him out into the garage. He led her over to a row of boxes. Something meowed from the uppermost one and Addie stopped in her tracks.

"We found her at a house fire, alone." Finn shoved his hands in his pockets and nodded toward the box.

Addie shot him a perplexed look before she glanced into the box. "Oh my God." She stared at the grey ball of fur. Deep blue eyes that matched her own widened and stared up at her. The kitten went up on her back two feet and peered over the edge of the box, meowing non stop. "A kitten?"

Finn rubbed the back of his neck. "You said you wanted one."

"Yes." Addie reached in and held the kitten to her face. "Hi, there, girl. You're so pretty." The kitten nuzzled her chin and she was lost. "I can't take her yet, not back to school."

"I can bring her by your place when you get home."

She glanced from the kitten to him, saw he was as surprised by the offer as she was. Something about the fact that he'd remembered she'd wanted a kitten, and thought of her when he saw one, made her thaw a little toward him. "Okay. I'll give you my number so you can get directions." He pulled out his phone and she rattled off her number.

"Okay." He shoved the phone back in his pocket and she watched the movement.

"Thank you." Addie set the kitten back in the box, her

heart breaking at the mewling cries. "I'll stop by the store on my way home and get what she needs."

He nodded but didn't say anything else. She wondered if he was rethinking his decision to bring the kitten to her apartment. Addie wasn't going to let him off easy though, if he wanted to change his mind, he'd have to tell her.

She left him standing in the garage and went back to the kids. Her heart beat wildly in her chest and she couldn't figure out why his little gesture affected her that much.

Chapter Six

Finn

He pulled into a free parking spot near Addie's apartment building and ran a hand down his face. What was he doing? This was bordering on insane, and he couldn't figure out why he'd offered to bring the kitten to her place. She could've come by the firehouse on her way home from school. But no, he'd opened his damn mouth and now here he was, a box with a kitten in it, preparing to head up to apartment 23.

Taking a deep breath, he got out. He found her apartment easily on the second floor and stood a minute before he knocked. There was no going back now.

She swung the door open and his heart stuttered. Her hair was in a messy pony-tail, she had no make up on, and she wore sweats and a t-shirt. His jeans suddenly felt too small.

"Hi." She stepped back.

He went inside, set the cardboard box on her counter. To calm himself down he looked around, noted that her place wasn't spotless. It fit her. "Nice place."

"Thanks." She reached into the box and scooped the kitten out. "Hey there, cutie pie. Ready to explore your new home?" She set the kitten on the carpet and watched it sniff at her feet and then move slowly around.

Not knowing what else to do, he just stood there.

"Want a beer?" Addie glanced at him, then pointed to the fridge. "I have Dos Equis, if you like that."

He nodded. Why didn't he just leave?

"Help yourself." She followed the kitten into the living room area.

Shrugging to himself, he gave up and went into the small kitchen and grabbed two beers from the fridge. He handed her one as he walked into the living room.

"Thanks. The kids loved the field trip, by the way. It's all they talked about for the rest of the day." She sat on the couch, gestured for him to join her.

"Good." God help him, but he couldn't think of anything else to say. She didn't seem to mind, because she kept talking.

"I haven't thought of a name for the little girl. What do you think?"

"Me?" Finn glanced at the little fur ball that crawled around her entertainment center. "I don't know."

She laughed at him and his abdomen tensed. "Nothing? No names come to mind?"

He felt foolish now that he couldn't think of something. He racked his brain for something that Addie would like. Something that would suit her. "Harlow."

She considered the name. "I love it. Her name is Harlow. I think it fits her." Addie stood and he watched the way she moved. "I'm going to show her the food and water bowl and her litter box." She picked Harlow up, giving him a good look at her ass in the sweatpants, and walked around the counter into the kitchen.

His hands fisted on his thighs. This was a bad idea. All he wanted to do was put his hands in her hair and kiss her until all she thought about was him. He didn't move though. He couldn't make himself leave, even though he thought about it.

"Have you had dinner?" She called from her little laundry room.

"No." He knew she was inviting him to stay, to eat with her. He could easily get up and leave, but he felt glued to the couch. His skin started to itch, to crawl, and he bit the inside of his cheek.

"Hey, are you okay?" Addie appeared next to him, sank down.

He hated seeing the worried look in her eyes, just like his sisters. "Fine."

Addie placed a hand on his.

The panic evaporated. Just like that, from the feel of her hand on his. His eyes widened as he looked into her calm face. There was no pity in her eyes, and that's what sold him.

He pulled her onto his lap, his hand going to the back of her neck. Her lips pressed to his before he could pull her closer and a thrill shot through him at her not being coy. She settled on top of him and dug her fingers into his hair.

His tongue slipped into her mouth, a teasing exploration, as one hand slid up her thigh to her waist. She nipped his lower lip and pressed closer to him. The center of her sweats rubbed against the bulge in jeans and he lost his breath for a second.

She smirked against his lips and rubbed herself against him, letting his tongue swipe over hers. His hands tightened on her waist when she pulled back a little.

"I have to eat something first. Just because you brought me a kitten doesn't mean I'm going to fall into bed with you. You have to buy me dinner a few times first." Addie slid off his lap.

He ran a hand through his hair, tried to get a handle on his breathing. Jesus Christ, that woman was a ball of fire.

"Do you want Chinese or Mexican?" She asked as she went to the menus that hung on her fridge.

His mind couldn't wrap itself around the question, so it took him a minute to answer. "Mexican."

"Cool, that's what I wanted." She brought the menu to him and a pad and pencil so he could write down his order.

If she saw his hand shaking a little when he reached for the stuff she didn't say anything about it, just went to get her cell. When she returned she took the paper from him and placed the order.

She sat close enough that their thighs touched and looked at him. "What made you be such an ass to me?"

He could tell by her tone that she wasn't being a whiny female, just curious about his actions, so he sighed. "It's my thing."

She arched a brow at him. "Your thing? Because giving me the kitten didn't seem like a very ass thing to do."

"Yeah, well, I knew you wanted it, so I brought it." He shifted on the couch. Talking about himself or his past was the last thing he wanted to do. She seemed to realize that and let the subject drop.

She picked up the remote to the TV. "What do you want to watch?"

Relief coursed through him at her change of subject. Most women would dig in and beg him to tell them about his past hurts and why he was this way. That's what made him leave them every time, why he focused on staying away from them. "You pick."

"I'll go easy on you and pick something not too girly." She went through the guide to the movie channels and found a comedy. "You like comedies?"

He did, actually. They were his favorite before. "Sure."

She set the remote down and put a pillow in her lap. Her fingertips played with the myriad buttons sewn onto the front and he got the feeling that she couldn't sit still for long. That doing stuff with her hands helped her to focus and concentrate.

Somehow he tore his stare from her and to the Adam Sandler comedy that flashed on the screen. He didn't really see any of it, only felt the warmth of her body as she sat beside him.

When the delivery man knocked on the door, Finn held his hand out to her. "I'll get it."

"Okay, thanks." Addie sat back.

Finn looked through the peephole before opening the

door. His adrenaline coursed through him, fast and quick, and he hated the fact that war had changed him this way. That he couldn't even answer a door without preparing to fight the person on the other side.

"Hey, man. It'll be 33.50." The blonde teenager held out the bags with the receipt stapled to it.

Finn set the bags on the ground beside him and reached into his back pocket for his wallet. He handed the kid $50 and told him to keep the change.

"Thanks, man." The kid grinned and walked back down the stairs.

"That was sweet." Addie stood by the counter with two plates and some utensils. "Do you want to eat at the bar or on the couch?"

"Doesn't matter."

Addie grabbed the plates and forks and took them to the coffee table. "Most of the time I eat here, since I don't have a table."

He didn't know how to reply so he carried the white plastic bags to the coffee table and sat on the couch. He wasn't trying to be rude by not talking. Sometimes he had a hard time forming words.

She grabbed her order, tucked her feet underneath her legs and started eating. He tried not to stare, but he loved the way she ate without worrying what she looked like. She clearly enjoyed her food.

His ex had eaten each bite so meticulously, always worried about getting food on her face or the weight she would gain. It drove him nuts. Didn't matter, though. He broke it off when he realized that everything she did made him crazy, and not in a good way.

"Are you going to eat?" Addie's voice broke him out of his reverie.

He blinked, realized he held the box in his hand but hadn't opened it. "Yeah." He cleared his throat, opened the box and dug in.

They sat in companionable silence, watching the movie, and eating. Harlow meowed at Finn's feet after he finished. He scooped her up and set her in his lap. He'd never really liked cats, but this one stared up at him with luminous blue eyes that reminded him of Addie. The kitten nuzzled his fingers and he ran his hand down her small body.

At the sound of purring, Addie grinned over at him. "Good to see you have a soft side."

His face cracked in a smile that felt weird on his face. "Do I seem like an ass all time?"

"Not all the time. You were sweet with Abigail today. If you hadn't, I'd have kicked your ass in the garage." Addie took a sip of her tea. "She's had a hard time with male figures in her life. Her dad died a few years ago, and her mom's boyfriends aren't always the best."

"That sucks for the girl." Finn was lucky on that front. He came from a big family, he had four sisters, two of which lived in Sanctuary Bay. That's the whole reason he moved here after leaving the Marines, to be with them.

"Yeah, well, life isn't always kind. I lucked out, but some of the people I know didn't. It breaks my heart."

He could hear the sincerity in her voice, she wasn't just saying it to say it. She truly felt for those people she knew.

At the end of the movie, Finn stood. It was too tempting sitting next to her, especially after her kiss. He needed to leave before he started something he wasn't entirely sure he wanted to continue.

"Thanks of dinner." Addie rose up on her tiptoes and brushed a kiss over the stubble on his cheek. "See ya."

He walked back to his truck, brushing his fingertips over the spot her lips touched. The heat of it stayed with him the entire way home.

Chapter Seven

Addie

"Hey, thanks for this." Addie sat on the stool in Victoria's kitchen the next morning. Halle sat next to her, a mimosa in hand.

"Sure. You said you needed to talk, so here we are." Victoria stood on the other side of the bar and took a sip of her mimosa.

Addie loved seeing the sparkle in her sister's eyes, the color in her cheeks. Being with Nick definitely looked good on her. "Where are Nick and the girls?"

"He took them to his mom's. They're going to go to the beach and I'll join them later." Victoria narrowed her eyes over the rim of her cup. "So, what's up?"

Addie sighed. "I met a guy."

Halle snickered into her cup. "You always meet guys."

"No, I *met* a guy." She stressed the word, knowing her sisters would get it.

Victoria nearly dropped her drink. "As in, you like him more than a one night stand kind of thing?"

"I haven't slept with him yet."

"Holy hell." Halle shook her head, amazement in her eyes. "That's not like you."

"Spill everything. Now." Victoria pulled a stool around and sat on it.

Addie felt her sisters' stares, knew they weren't going to let this go. It was why she came, right? To get this off her chest. She launched into the story of how she and Finn met, the sports bar, the field trip and the kitten. She even told them about the kiss she put on him.

"You didn't go any further than that?" Halle asked.

"No." Addie spun her glass around in her hands. "I wanted to, trust me. He's hot and tattooed. But he has a past, something happened to him. I can see it in his eyes."

"Everyone has a past, honey." Victoria laid a hand over hers.

Addie held her sister's hand for a minute. "I know, but do I want to deal with that? I'm not the type of person to heal other people. I love 'em and leave 'em, not stick around."

She saw the look that Halle and Victoria shared. She didn't bristle about it, she knew they cared about her.

"What?"

"This guy has you tied up in knots. I've never known you to even notice a guy's feelings that way." Victoria held up a hand when Addie opened her mouth to defend herself. "Sweetie, it's not a bad thing. You're just you, and this guy has you seeing things you don't normally see."

"I don't want to see things." Addie's shoulders slumped. "I want things the way they are. I want my independence, and I'm not looking for anything more."

"Did he ask for anything more?" Halle asked.

"No, no he didn't." Addie faced her own brutal honesty. "I'm afraid that I will."

Now both her sisters' eyes widened.

"I know. It's not me at all. There's something about him, I don't know what it is." Addie couldn't steady her mixed emotions. "It scares the hell out of me."

Halle put an arm around her waist, pulled her close. "Don't let it. Look at Victoria. Look how happy she is. That can happen to you, too."

"It can happen to you, Halle." Victoria put in.

Halle tensed beside her and this time Addie pulled her into a hug. "I can hit him again, if you want."

Halle moved away, shook her head. "No, I'm okay. I've had time to get over it."

Addie and Victoria shared the look this time.

"It's only been three months. It took me over a year to really get over what Roger did and he didn't cheat like Trevor did." Victoria's eyes misted for her sister.

"It's okay, I'm okay." Halle smiled at them, but Addie saw the strain.

Not for the first time Addie wanted to hunt Trevor and his little whore, Jenna, down and beat the hell out of them. It would make her feel better, that's for sure.

"Did Luke invite you two to his game party Saturday?"

Addie noticed Halle perk up a bit when Victoria said Luke's name. "Yep, I'll be there and I'll drag Halle kicking and screaming."

Halle pushed Addie's shoulder. "I'm not a total hermit. I'll go and I'll even drive myself."

"Got something to prove?" Addie teased, and Halle's answering smile cheered her some.

§§

Addie smiled at her nieces as they walked into their house. They were already gearing up to beat her in bowling on the Wii and she shook her head. How could they possible love playing that game all the time? It didn't matter, she'd play as many times as they wanted just to see them happy.

Nick and Victoria were both working late tonight, Victoria at a staging for a rental house and Nick at a client's house, trying to wrap up his contracting work before the happy couple returned from their honeymoon in France.

Addie dropped her purse on the table by the door, removed her black flats and waited on the girls to get it set up. They chattered about their day to each other as they grabbed the remotes and came to stand next to the couch.

"You ready?" Lucia quirked an eyebrow at her.

It reminded Addie so much of Victoria that she was momentarily stunned. "You bet." She recovered, sent the girls a wink.

As they played, Addie kept thinking about Finn. She hadn't seen him since last Friday night. A few times she almost picked up her phone and texted him and that bothered her. She wasn't the type to go after a man, they came to her. Just the thought that she was already weakening toward him pissed her off. It wasn't his fault, she knew, but that didn't stop her from being pissed at him. She was a woman and that gave her the right.

After a few rounds, Helena took the wrist strap off and put the controller up. "I need to start this paper. I told the teacher I'd have it finished in a few days." She hugged Addie close. "Say 'bye before you leave."

"Of course." Addie snuggled her closer before Helena walked away.

"I'm hungry. Want a snack?" Lucia gestured toward the kitchen.

Addie heard the change in her tone of voice, saw the way her hands messed with the ends of her pony-tail. "Yeah, let's get one." Something was bothering her.

They picked crackers with cheese and bacon bits, and Lucia sat while Addie arranged everything on a plate and brought it to the bar. Lucia nibbled on a cracker and Addie waited for her to say what was wrong. It didn't take long.

"When did you lose your virginity?"

Addie coughed on the cracker, had to swig almost a whole glass of water. Not just to clear her throat but to organize her thoughts. Lucia watched her, hands twisted in her lap, until Addie set the glass down. "Why are you asking that?" She racked her brain for reasons, none of them good.

"Some of the girls on the cheer squad have already lost theirs," Lucia whispered.

Addie forced the question out even if she didn't really want to know. "Are you one of them?"

Lucia's gaze snapped to hers. "No!"

Relief coursed through and almost knocked Addie to her knees. She wasn't prepared for this. What was she supposed to say? Did she need to tell Victoria? "Good. Is that the only reason you're asking?"

Lucia cut her eyes to the left, shrugged.

Addie's stomach clenched. "Lucia." She reached for her niece's hand. "Why are you asking? You know you can talk to me about anything."

"It's just...there's this guy, Connor. And he's really sweet and we've been talking," Lucia said. "But he's starting to talk about...that...and I don't know what to do."

Jesus. Sweet Jesus. Addie had no idea what to say. Isn't this a conversation a girl had with her mother? Then she thought, did she talk to her mother about this? Hell no. "What do you want to do?"

"I don't know. I like him, but I'm not sure I like him that much."

"Is he pressuring you?" Addie would kick a little boy's ass in a heart beat.

"No, just talking about it. I never really say anything back, but some of the girls on the squad say that if I don't do it, he'll stop talking to me."

These girls were thirteen years old. Why were they

worried about this now? Was this really when it started? Addie's heart squeezed when Lucia looked up, tears shimmering and threatening to fall. This was serious. "Why don't you talk to your mom about this?"

Lucia wiped a hand over her eyes and red nose. "No, you have to promise you won't tell her. Promise!"

Addie sighed. She hated the position she was in right now. She wasn't sure not telling Victoria was the right thing to do, but on the other hand she didn't want to betray Lucia's trust. "Okay. I promise. Now, let me tell you something. Those girls don't know what they're talking about. That type of...relation...between people is special. Especially your first time. Don't let yourself get pressured into it with a boy you barely know."

"I know." Lucia sniffled, grabbed a paper towel to wipe her eyes and nose. "I won't do anything like that. I'm not ready."

Addie nudged the plate of crackers over to her. "Hungry?"

"Yeah." Lucia's smile was shaky but Addie was sure she'd gotten through to her.

How was she going to face Victoria with this secret knowledge she promised not to tell? She'd never kept anything a secret from her sisters, and didn't want to start now, but she promised. This was going to kill her inside, she just knew it. And when Victoria found out about it and somehow figured Addie knew before her and didn't say anything? Victoria would kill her on the outside.

Addie ate the crackers with Lucia in an uncomfortable silence until they were gone. When Victoria came home, Addie made an excuse and left. She couldn't face her yet.

Chapter Eight

Finn

On the way to the game party he stopped to pick up chips and dip. He tried to force his nervousness down and told himself that it would only be for a little while.

Luke's apartment was on the first floor and he knocked. The door swung open and his pulse stumbled.

"Hey." Addie looked as surprised as he did and her cheeks flushed.

Why did he think that was sexy as hell? "Hey."

They stood like that for a few moments until another woman pulled Addie out of the way.

"You have to excuse her, she was raised with cave men." The girl resembled Addie, but had her dark hair cut in a bob and whiskey brown eyes. "I'm Halle."

"Finn."

He caught the raised eyebrow Halle turned on Addie, but didn't think much of it.

"Come in." Addie gestured for him to enter and took the grocery bags he carried.

Finn shut the door behind him. Voices floated in from the living room and he tensed. He couldn't do this, he couldn't. The crowded room made his skin crawl.

A soft hand touched his forearm, right over his Celtic shield tattoo, and the crawling sensation drowned underneath the heat from her touch. Addie looked at him, questions in her eyes that he didn't want to answer.

"I'll introduce you to everyone." Addie handed the bags to Halle and she took them to the kitchen.

He followed her into the living room, which was sizable for an apartment. Several people stood and others sat in chairs and on the sectional. Luke stood, looking between Finn and Addie.

"Finn, glad you could make it." Luke clapped him on the shoulder. "I see you've met Addie."

Finn just nodded, ignored Addie's puzzled look.

"Halle was at the door with her, Addie's sister. Victoria," he pointed to another look alike of Addie's, who sat on the couch beside a guy who looked like Luke. "And that's my brother, Nick. My mom is on the couch with them and Victoria's daughters, Lucia and Helena."

Finn nodded to each person, the pressure thickening on

his chest. This was a family thing so far and he felt like he was intruding. Had Addie told Luke to invite him? No, that didn't make any sense, they barely knew each other when Luke had invited him.

"Dear, why don't you have a seat over here." Cecelia waved him to a chair. "Thanks for bringing something, although you didn't have to."

"Yeah, Mom made enough food to feed a third world country." Addie teased.

"Thanks, ma'am." Finn slowly sat.

Cecelia laughed. "No ma'am here. You call me Cecelia."

"How do you and Addie know each other?" Luke suddenly asked.

Finn tensed until Addie punched Luke in the shoulder. "He's a firefighter. Remember, we took the third graders to see the firehouse last week? Lay off."

Luke rubbed his shoulder. "Are you sure you don't want to join the fight scene?"

Cecelia cleared her throat and Luke held up his hands. "Joking."

"Want a beer?" Nick stood, asking Finn.

"Sure." Finn tried not to fist his hands on the arms of the chair. They seemed like really nice people, but being around this many in such a social setting, with them being a family, made it hard to relax. He tried not to follow Addie's movements with his gaze, but that was hard, too.

"Here you go." Nick handed him the beer, already open.

"Thanks." Finn had seen him around the gym from time to time, saw him and his brother spar.

A knock sounded on the door and Luke rose to get it. "I think that's Matt and Rhona."

Luke came back into the living room, followed by a very pregnant woman and another guy he'd seen at the gym, a trainer. When he saw Luke giving introductions again, and that the couple was obviously not family also, Finn relaxed a little. He didn't feel like he was intruding as much.

"How long have you been in Sanctuary Bay, Finn?" Cecelia asked from her chair near his.

"I moved here a few months ago for my sisters, ma-- Cecelia." He cut off the ma'am just in time. Her lips quirked and it reminded him of Addie's smile.

"That's very nice. How many sisters do you have?"

"Four, although only two live here."

"Mom, stop interrogating him." Addie shot her mom a look. "He's a guest."

Cecelia smiled at her. "I'm not interrogating him."

"You kind of are." Victoria told her with an apologetic look. "He shouldn't have to tell you his life story."

"Okay, I know when I'm beat." Cecelia laughed at them.

"Game's almost on," Wes said. "Let's get the food together."

Cecelia and Charlotte both stood, and both waved Wes to stay seated.

"We'll get it," Charlotte told them.

Finn didn't miss the worried looks Nick and Luke shared and he took a second look at Charlotte. She looked a little tired, but not overly so, so maybe the boys were overprotective of their mom. Then he stood so Rhona could have his seat. Now that he had no idea where to stand or what to do, he stood off to the side of the room awkwardly.

Luke's nieces were giggling on the couch, whispering to each other, and to their mom and Nick. He wondered if he'd have children now if his relationship had went the way he wanted with his ex. Mia had been too wild to settle down though.

"You're thinking too hard, not having fun." Addie leaned on the wall beside him. She tapped her beer to his. "Lose the pensive expression."

"Okay." He tried not to think about anything, which

was easy when Addie stared up at him with those dark blue eyes. His body responded to her closeness and he suddenly needed to think about anything *but* her. Because right now, all he could think about was her lips pressed to his the other night. "How is Harlow?"

Her eyes sparkled. "Good. I had to buy a smaller litter box. She couldn't get into the other one, so I'll save that one for when she gets bigger. She's just a fluffy mess of cuteness." She tucked a piece of hair behind her ear and his gaze followed the delicate curve of her neck. "Thanks for bringing her to me."

"You're welcome."

"Sorry about mom. She doesn't mean to interrogate, she just loves to know about people."

Finn lifted a shoulder. "It's okay, she didn't bother me."

"Four sisters? I've always wondered what it would be like to have a brother." Addie glanced toward Luke and Nick and he did, too. Both of them watched him with narrowed eyes. Addie glared at them and they suddenly had something else to watch. "I guess I know now, don't I?"

"I guess you do." Finn smiled and again his mouth stretched uncomfortably. How did she manage to make him do that? "What does that feel like? My sisters complain about it constantly."

"I'm getting used to it. I'm the one who usually takes care of my sisters, because they're both sweet and gentle." Addie looked back at him as Luke changed the channel to the game and turned it up. "It's nice to have some men to help with it."

Finn figured she handled herself well enough and didn't need the men to help her, but he felt better about Addie having brothers to look after her.

"Let's get some chairs from the kitchen." Addie walked off, leaving him to follow.

They settled beside the sectional in the wooden chairs and before he could lean back against the hard wood, Charlotte handed him a pillow.

"For your back, sweetie," she said before handing one to Addie.

"Thank you." Finn found the smile came easy when Charlotte patted his shoulder. Her touch was gentle and sweet, motherly. He hadn't seen his own mother since he moved and homesickness thickened in his chest.

As time passed, he found himself relaxed and smiling more. Addie teased him just as mercilessly as she did the others, and so did the rest of her family. They included him, Matt, and Rhona in everything and the moms doted on the pregnant girl like she was their own. He found himself enjoying watching Addie around her family. It was different from the wild child act that she had at the bar. Seeing all the different aspects to her surprised him.

Holy shit. He had to stop that train of thought now. For one, he wasn't settling down because he had too many issues on his own, and for two, she was a wild child and he wasn't looking to date someone like that. Not after Mia.

When Addie offered him chips, he took a paper plate and set some on there, grabbed some dip. The football game caught his attention, as much as it was able with Addie right next to him, and he focused on it. He didn't want to be distracted by her, didn't want to be attracted.

Chapter Nine

Addie

When Finn started to act distant toward her again she wondered what made him suddenly change back to the ass he'd been in the beginning. He quit talking to her, preferring to be silent or chat with Nick, Luke, or their parents.

She couldn't handle his back and forth, hot-cold attitude toward her. Normally when a guy acted this way she ignored them back but she found it hard. He'd smiled today, freely, and it didn't look like his face would crack from it. Hell, it had been such a surprise to see him when she'd opened the door that her brain had automatically frozen. Thank God Halle saved her from completely embarrassing herself.

Now he sat beside her, smile gone unless he spoke with someone else. She racked her brain to figure out if she'd said something to offend him, or been a general bitch, but she couldn't figure it out as much as she tried. Maybe she should stop worrying about his attitude and enjoy the time spent with her family. She loved hanging out with them and wouldn't let him ruin it.

She turned her attention to Lucia, the girl was just as upbeat as ever, laughing with Nick and his mom, with her grandparents. No hint of what she and Addie talked about the other day. Addie tried not to focus on that, because that was something else that could suck the fun out of the day. She wasn't a big fan of sports, but she was a big fan of her family, so she didn't mind watching it for a little while.

The debate over whether or not to tell Victoria about what she'd discussed with Lucia rose in her mind, battering at her. Addie mentally shook her head, turned to Halle, and smiled. "Who do you think is going to win?"

"I have no idea." Halle smirked at her. "And neither do you."

Addie watched Halle's gaze drift to Luke, before it snapped back to the TV. Her sister was interested in Nick's brother, even if she didn't realize it yet. How odd would that be, for two sisters to fall for two brothers? Addie didn't care as long as Luke didn't break Halle's heart.

Throughout the game, her friends and family cheered at every touchdown or booed at every misstep. She tried to follow what was going on, but every time Finn moved, her attention automatically focused on him, even if it was only in her peripheral vision.

Her mind knew that she should just drop him, ignore him and his asshole attitude, but her body wanted to experience more of what happened during the kiss. He lit every nerve in her body on fire. No other man had woken her body like that. Sure, she'd enjoyed the time spent with the other guys, but nothing compared to what happened with that one kiss.

Helena came and sat with her in the chair for a little while and they talked about her math club at school. Luckily boys didn't interest her as much as they did Lucia. Addie could breathe a sigh of relief on that one. That's all they needed, both girls interested in boys at the same time. Lucia was enough for now.

Addie wondered if she discussed it with Halle if Lucia would freak out. Lucia didn't tell her she couldn't talk to Halle about it, right? As long as Halle swore not to tell Victoria, she could get this off her chest and get some advice about how to help Lucia.

That's what she'd do. Tonight, she'd get Halle over to her apartment and discuss it.

§§

"This kitten is so cute!" Halle nuzzled nose to nose with Harlow, then moved her to the crook of her neck.

Addie heard the kitten purring from where she stood behind the bar, pouring them both a glass of wine. They'd need it.

"And Finn gave her to you?" Halle quirked an eyebrow.

"Yes, after he heard me saying that I wanted one at the sports bar." Addie pushed Halle's wine glass in her direction. "But don't read anything into it. He's so hot and cold, I don't know what to make of him."

"I think he's interested."

"Really?" Addie put a hand on her hip, gestured with the wine glass. "He barely talked to me at Luke's today. Not that I'm whining or anything, I hate when girls do that." She took a quick sip. "He gets me so unsettled. I hate it."

"You need someone who unsettles you." Halle smiled over at her. "That's the point. If you felt nothing, or just went through the motions, it wouldn't mean anything. You go for guys that are passive, that don't challenge you because you're scared to commit. Scared of getting hurt. But you know what? Who isn't?"

"I didn't ask you over to talk about Finn." Addie hated

the snap in her voice, but even talking about Finn made her edgy.

Halle took it in stride and Addie loved that about her. Halle could tell when she struck a nerve and didn't push. "What did you ask me over for?"

"Lucia." Addie took a deep breath, prayed she was making the right decision by telling Halle. "You have to promise that what we discuss is just between me and you. You can't tell Mom and you definitely, absolutely can't tell Victoria."

"Sounds serious." Halle nodded, eyes somber. "I promise not to speak a word."

"Okay." Addie took a longer sip of wine. "Lucia told me that her boyfriend wants to sleep with her."

"What?" Halle almost dropped the wine glass and Harlow jerked. "Sleep with...she's only thirteen, what the hell?"

"Exactly." Addie nodded. "But Lucia doesn't want to take that step, thank God. The thing is, all her cheerleader friends have already lost their V-card and are trying to peer pressure Lucia into doing it, too."

"Oh my God. Are you sure we don't want to talk to Victoria about this? This is serious."

"I know." Addie sighed. "Lucia made me swear not to

tell Victoria. To the point of tears. That's why I'm telling you. I need to know what's the right thing to do."

"When you were talking to Lucia, did it seem like she would cave?"

"She wants to wait, but is caught in the dilemma of him leaving her for someone who'll give him what he wants, or her friends leaving her out because she won't do it."

"Jesus, these girls are too young. Why are they even thinking about that right now?" Halle put Harlow on the floor. "I don't want to scare her again when if I freak out some more."

"I don't know, it blows my mind." Addie drained her wine glass and went to feed Harlow. "Should we tell Victoria?"

Halle bit her lip. "If we do, we'll break Lucia's trust and she won't tell you anything again."

"Does this warrant that, though?" Addie stepped back to the bar. "Is this one of those times we need to tell?"

"This may be one of the hardest decisions I've ever had to make, and I've had to make some truly hard ones lately." Halle set her empty wine glass on the bar. "Let's think about it tonight, both sleep on it. We can decide in the morning. I don't want to rush our decision and make the wrong one."

"Okay, that sounds better than anything I could think of." Addie placed both of their wine glasses in the sink, hugged Halle as she left, and then sat on the couch. It was a Saturday night, but she didn't feel like going out. Gemma and Autumn had both texted her a few times in disbelief, so she finally told them she wasn't feeling well.

It was odd for her not to go out on weekends, to find someone to have fun with. Tonight she didn't feel like going on the hunt or playing the game. She wanted to curl up on the couch, watch mindless TV, and cuddle with Harlow.

Flipping through channels, she decided to watch a reality TV show about couples finding the perfect house. She never really wanted a house, didn't want to worry about the upkeep of a lawn or cleaning a bigger space. Although seeing some of the ones on TV, she might change her mind.

She really needed to decide what to do about Lucia's problem. She tried to put herself in Victoria's shoes, imagining herself with a daughter and her having the same problem as Lucia. Would she want to know what was going on with her?

Hell yeah she would.

There, decision made. She'd let Halle come to her own decision and text her in the morning.

Chapter Ten

Finn

His sisters finally invited him over. He wondered what took them so long, but decided he'd ask when he got inside. They lived in a little house near the outskirts of town, which only took him five minutes to get to from the station. As he was about to get out of the car, his phone rang. This time he didn't hang up, the unease getting stronger. "Who is this? What the hell do you want?"

A muffled voice and static reached his ears. "I want you."

Finn looked at the phone but the number was blocked. When he put the phone back to his ear, the dial tone buzzed again. What the fuck was going on? Right now he wanted to focus on his sisters, so he ignored it for now.

Kelsey opened the door before he knocked and jumped on him. "I've missed you so much."

His arms went around her, his sisters being just about

the only people he let touch him. Besides Addie now. He pushed the wild girl out of his mind and focused on his next-to-youngest sister.

After hugging him for a few seconds she led him to the living room. "Jenna's at work, so I called you."

He heard what she didn't say. Their wild sister didn't want him coming over. Jenna always pushed her older siblings away because she thought they didn't approve of her, that they'd lecture her the entire time. It was impossible not to want to steer her in a different direction with the way she lived her life. It surprised him that she didn't mind Kelsey staying with her.

He glanced at Kelsey, saw she glowed with happiness. She was the exact opposite of Jenna, sweet and caring. Her blonde hair was long and wavy and her blue eyes shone with the goodness inside of her.

"Want coffee? I made some when I called." Kelsey pulled down two mugs, not waiting on his answer.

"Sure." He took a seat at the small square table and watched her move around, fluttering nervously. "Kelsey."

She stopped, turned and looked at him. "Hmm?"

"What's wrong?" He pinned her with a serious gaze, knowing she couldn't withstand the look.

"Stop, you know I hate that." Kelsey quickly made the

coffee and set his mug in front of him before sitting. When he didn't stop, she sighed. "Okay, fine."

He sipped his coffee, holding back a smug smirk.

"I don't want to be a tattle tell, I don't want to make Jenna mad by telling you what happened." She tapped her fingertips on the mug.

"What happened?" His stomach sank. With Jenna it could be anything from drugs to men.

Kelsey groaned, then said, "She slept with her boss a few months ago and his wife caught them at the office."

"What the fuck?" Finn's grip tightened on his mug. What the hell was Jenna's problem?

"She said all the other girls were doing it, which I know is not a good excuse." Kelsey's shoulder lifted in a shrug. "The wife divorced him. Jenna's still working there, and I think she's still sleeping with him."

"Jesus Christ. What is wrong with that girl?" Finn wanted to beat some sense into her. "How could she do that?"

"You know how she is, Finn. It's why she moved away from everyone. She doesn't want anyone interfering in the way she does things." Kelsey's blue eyes watched him over the mug. "I'm telling you because I think she might listen to you."

"She won't. It'll pass through her selfish brain, and she'll go right back to it. She's lucky the wife didn't beat the hell out of her."

"True, but you know that wouldn't stop her. She doesn't care about anything but what she gets out of it. She doesn't care who she hurts, as long as she gets what she wants."

"Is that why it took you so long to invite me over? Because Jenna didn't want me to find out?" He was seriously going to have a talk with his youngest sister and she'd listen whether she wanted to or not. If she kept this up, she was going to ruin her life.

Kelsey's cheeks tinged pink and she nodded. "I didn't want her mad at me."

Jenna mad was like an F4 tornado, she ripped through you until there was nothing left. Kelsey wouldn't want to deal with that, being a non-confrontational person. He'd handle it, and if Jenna went after Kelsey he'd handle that, too.

"I understand. She can be a real bitch when she's angry." Finn changed the subject, wanting Kelsey to relax. "So, what's up with you?"

"Nothing. I found some buyers for my paintings, so I was able to get some more supplies. I need to find a studio or build one onto the house to have more space. Right now it's in my room and it's cramped in there."

"How much will it cost?"

"No, you're not buying it for me." Kelsey pointed a finger at him.

"I have plenty of money just sitting there, I'm not using it."

"I want to do this on my own, Finn. Please. I have to prove to myself that I can." Kelsey stared pointedly at him until he answered.

"Fine. Fine, I understand." Finn sighed. He really wanted to help her, and that money was just sitting there. He couldn't stand the thought of using it for himself, thought of it more as blood money.

"How are you doing?" She reached across the table and placed her hand on his Celtic shield tattoo. She knew why he'd gotten it, who he'd gotten it with. Knew that he still grieved for his best friend even if he didn't show it.

Finn couldn't talk over the lump in his throat that suddenly formed. Kelsey was the only one who would truly understand, she'd loved Isaac from the time they were teenagers and had planned on marrying him when he came back from overseas. He understood her need to prove to herself that she was okay. Her hand tightened on his and a few tears fell down her cheeks.

He never could stand the sight of her crying. He tugged on her hand, getting her to come over to him. He held her while she sobbed, the front of his shirt getting soaked. If a few tears fell from his eyes, he ignored them. Losing Isaac was the hardest thing he'd ever gone through and leaving Mia soon after, even if it was his idea, put his emotions behind an impenetrable wall. But here, with Kelsey, knowing she was going through the same thing, made it easier to let the walls slip a little.

When they finished, he asked, "How about I mow the lawn and do a little yard work? I'm off today and it could use it."

Kelsey nodded, used a paper towel to wipe her eyes and nose. "Okay. I'm going to go paint. I need to right now."

For as long as he could remember, Kelsey used painting to work through her emotions. He'd give her the silence and room to do it while he worked through his emotions a different way. He went to the back yard and into the little wooden shed that held the mower, weed eater, and shears. The mower started right up and he cut the grass.

It wasn't long before sweat dripped in his eyes, down his back, and soaked the front of his shirt. The hard work made his muscles burn, but it was a good burn. Feeling like he accomplished something helped keep his demons at bay.

No cloud cover gave him a reprieve from the hot sun and he wished he had some sunscreen. His neck and arms burned hot from the rays.

When he finished with mowing the front and back, he grabbed the weed eater and got the grass by the sidewalk, driveway, and mail box. By the time he was done with that, it was lunch time.

Kelsey waved him in, fed him a sandwich and sweet, iced tea before he went back out and cut back some of the limbs and bushes. He stood and looked over the front of their house. It needed a refresher of white paint, but it fit them. A great starter house for his sisters.

He put everything back in the shed and went inside to say goodbye. Kelsey was in her room, sitting at an easel, brows furrowed in concentration. The face of the man she painted wasn't finished, but the warm brown eyes held a hint of mischief. She painted Isaac in his uniform, the day they both went to war.

He left without disturbing her and headed back to the station for a much needed shower. His heart ached from seeing the painting of his best friend. Isaac had been full of humor and life and watching him die had taken a devastating toll on Finn. A part of him died with Isaac that day.

After his shower he checked in with the chief to see if he needed to do anything. After telling Finn that the investigators confirmed what he thought, an arsonist lit the beach house on fire, Chief waved him out of the office with an order to relax. If only the chief knew that he couldn't do that, not anymore. His body stayed on constant alert, like he hadn't acclimated to civilian life yet. He wasn't sure he ever would. Every shadow, every noise in the dark reminded him of the worst time of his life. He couldn't block it out, couldn't give that part of himself resolution.

Just to give it a try, he sat down on the couch and turned the TV on. The other guys were out grocery shopping for the station and since it was his day off, he technically wasn't suppose to be here. But, he had no where else to go. No apartment or house yet, and soon Kelsey would start wondering why he didn't have one.

He couldn't bring himself to settle down that much. To make that big decision to stay. Not that he didn't want to, it just felt like too big of a move right now. Why should he have a place to live, be happy, when his best friend was ashes in the wind? No, it was better that he drift, too.

Chapter Eleven

Addie

She was running late. Gemma had asked Addie to meet her and Carter at a seafood hole-in-the-wall that the girls liked. She'd rushed home from school and threw on a pair of shorts and a spaghetti-strapped shirt. The heat was unbelievable and she didn't want to wear more than she had to. Her hair was up in a messy bun because the humidity had it frizzing like crazy and it had a mind of its own.

The smell of fried shrimp and potatoes rose on the hot air in the parking lot and her stomach growled. She was looking forward to some good food. When she entered the restaurant, she immediately saw Finn sitting at the table with Gemma and Carter. Her pace stumbled a bit. That witch had tricked her into a double date and she could tell by the surprise on Finn's face, he hadn't known about it either.

Gemma jumped out of her seat when Addie spun on her

sandals and went out the door.

"Addie, wait!" Gemma ran around in front of her, forcing her to stop in the gravel of the parking lot.

"Damn it, Gemma. You know he's an asshole. Why are you doing this?" Addie couldn't keep the venom from her voice. She *hated* being set up.

"I know, I do." Gemma placed her palms together, pleading. "Carter says it's because of his past and we should give him a chance. It's important to Carter that Finn be included in stuff."

"Stuff includes a double date? Seriously?" Addie went to move around Gemma but the girl was a ninja in high heels and blocked her again. "Gemma."

"Please. Addie, just give him a chance." Gemma reached for her hand, started to pull her toward the restaurant. "Just tonight. He did bring you a kitten."

Addie sighed, feeling the fight leave her. She couldn't resist Gemma when the girl practically begged her to come inside. "Fine. But if he's an ass, just once, I'm gone and he can pay the bill."

"Okay." Gemma hopped once, beaming. "You're awesome."

"I know." Addie shrugged off her irritation, went inside behind Gemma. "Hey, Carter. Finn."

Carter pulled out both of the girl's chairs and pushed them to the table. Addie cast a glance at Finn and saw he was as uncomfortable as she was. Her first instinct was to make him comfortable, it's what she did with everyone, but she held back a little at first.

"What are you guys drinking?" A waitress came over. She took their drink orders before walking to the back.

"How was work, Addie?" Carter asked when the waitress left.

"Good, third graders have insane energy." Addie picked up a menu. She ate here all the time, but sometimes wanted something different. She quickly decided on grilled tilapia, potatoes, and a salad.

"I have a nephew that age, and he's non stop. I swear he runs in his sleep." Carter laughed.

Addie watched him stare at Gemma adoringly, and couldn't decide if she was annoyed still or not. "What's his name?"

"Trent. He's my sister's kid. They live in Orange Beach, AL. My sister owns a yoga-Pilates gym down there," Carter told them. "Her husband works for a shipbuilder."

"Why are you so far away from them?" Addie asked, starting to get curious about the guy who held Gemma's heart.

"We're actually from NYC, but Sasha met her husband in Virginia when he was in the Coast Guard. I'm not exactly sure why they picked the Gulf Coast, but they love it." Carter shrugged. "As long as she's happy, I'm happy. I'm planning to go visit her soon."

Finn stayed silent throughout the conversation and Addie kept glancing at him. He still looked tense in his chair. Nothing like he'd been at her apartment. Definitely not like he'd been when he'd kissed her back. Heat flooded her cheeks and she tore her gaze from him. Why didn't she want to play with fire like she normally did?

Because she wasn't sure she could take the heat. Not his brand of it. He intrigued her to the point that she didn't think clearly and she couldn't take him looking so uncomfortable, either. "Finn, what are you going to order?"

His green eyes met hers, intense and stormy. "Not sure."

She quirked an eyebrow. "Seafood, I assume. I'm getting the grilled tilapia with potatoes and salad." She pinned him with her teacher's gaze, waiting on him to answer.

He sat up straighter, pulled a menu to him. "What's good?"

Finally, he was engaging with her. She knew this place.

"Do you like fried shrimp?"

"Sure." His gaze drifted over her and that fire lit up again.

"Their fried shrimp is awesome, and get French fries with it. Oh, and the Remoulade sauce is great, too." Addie let her stare roam over him in answer. She didn't mind a little harmless flirting once in a while.

"Okay." He leaned back in his chair and Addie couldn't help but watch the way he moved. He intrigued her, one of the only guys to not fall directly in her bed, and she wanted to know what made him tick, why he rebuffed her. Not in a whiny-hurt way, but with serious curiosity.

The waitress came back and they put in their orders, Finn going with what Addie suggested. More people filed in and sat down and conversations rose and fell in the warm air of the restaurant.

Was the air warm because it bordered the ocean, or was it warm because Finn sat at the table with her?

Halle was right, he did bring her a sweet kitten, but did that mean she wanted to get involved with him? He wasn't like the usual guys she met, she could sense something had hurt him and it shimmered just below his facade of quietness. Would she want to be there when that wall cracked?

"In a few weekends, Carter and I want to rent a condo off the beach in Virginia. His sister is thinking of joining us. We wanted to see if you and Finn wanted to come along. Autumn is coming, along with Caleb." Gemma flashed Addie a you-better look.

Addie wondered when Gemma and Carter had become a *we*. "I'm in. I haven't been to those beaches and could use a vacation from Sanctuary Bay for a weekend."

Finn shifted in his chair.

"Come on, Finn. You can stand to be in my company for a weekend, right? Or would being around me constantly for three days tempt you too much?" She winked at him.

His lips twitched and Addie knew he'd heard the dare in her voice. "I think I can resist." He looked over at Carter and Gemma. "Just let me know when you have the weekend planned and I'll let Chief know."

"'Atta boy." Addie laughed, glad that he was showing some type of emotion. She'd only known him for a few weeks, but seeing him in that numb mode bothered her. She didn't want to analyze why, though.

"Okay, it's about a seven hour trip. We can all ride together and meet his sister and her family." Gemma's eyes lit up. "It's going to be so much fun." She'd already pulled her phone out and scrolled through Google to find them a condo.

"She doesn't waste a second, does she?" Carter cast Gemma another adoring look.

"Nope, never. She's a planner." Addie grinned.

The waitress brought their food and Addie waited for Finn to take his first bite.

"Damn, this is good." Finn nodded toward Addie. "Thanks."

She smiled at him before starting on her tilapia. This place made the best seafood as far as she was concerned and was glad that he liked what she suggested. She wanted to suggest other things, like her, but still wasn't sure if she wanted to take that step. Maybe she'd decide on their vacation.

Carter and Gemma kept the conversation going and Addie jumped in a few times when she had something to say. Finn stayed quiet after that, murmuring when someone asked him a direct question, which Gemma did a few times to pull him into the conversation.

When they finished their meals, the waitress brought the tickets, and only set down two. Obviously she thought Addie and Finn were a couple.

Addie reached for it, but Finn stopped her by placing a hand on hers. "I've got it."

Addie shook her head, pink tingeing her cheeks at the electric rush from his touch. "You don't have to."

"I don't mind." His crooked half-smile shot straight to her heart. Each and every time he smiled it was like a direct line to a transformer, her skin electrified.

"You're going to be stubborn, aren't you?" She tilted her head to the side, weirdly happy that he hadn't moved his hand yet.

His fingers brushed hers as he pulled the check from under her hand. "Yep."

Carter cleared his throat, making Addie jump. For just a few moments, she'd forgotten about Gemma and Carter.

Yeah, Finn was definitely dangerous.

Chapter Twelve

Finn

He grabbed the dumbbells off the shelf and started doing bicep curls. Looking around the gym, he saw that it was mostly packed in the middle of the day. For some reason, he didn't want to work out at the station, preferring to get out for a while. Being at the station reminded him of Addie, and he couldn't focus, or sleep, with her on his mind.

Especially with dinner the other night. She'd playfully teased him, shooting him heated glances that had him so hard he was afraid to get up from the table when the meal was over. He really needed to get her off his mind. Maybe working himself into a sweat and making his body regret it moved would help. Maybe if he worked out so hard that his brain quit functioning, he could sleep without seeing her face first.

Every word she spoke that night had his eyes lingering

on her lush mouth.

He cursed under his breath when he realized he was thinking about her again. The damn woman had a way of sneaking into his thoughts and staying there, as stubborn that way as she was in real life. The challenge of her, of her stubbornness, had a weird way of turning him on. He'd thought after Mia's wild ways he'd never look at another wild girl again.

But he couldn't take his eyes off of Addie. Or his mind, and he knew from the kiss that night, he'd have a hard time keeping his hands off her, too.

"Glad you made it to the game the other night, Finn." Nick walked up.

Finn stopped his curls, set the weights at his feet. "Yeah, me too."

Luke joined them and Finn automatically tensed.

"Relax, Finn." Luke sent him a grin that took the fight out of Finn.

"Sure, yeah." Finn nodded. "Habit."

"Are you dating Addie?" Nick crossed his arms, face solemn.

Finn tensed again. "No."

"Doesn't look like it. Matt saw you with her and some friends at the seafood place the other night. Said you two looked pretty chummy." Luke's stare bore into him.

Shit, why had he thought Addie having guys to look after her was a good thing? "Nothing's going on."

The brothers' stares didn't relent and sweat beaded on Finn's back. Christ, were they going to challenge him right here? He didn't feel like getting into a fight with guys he was beginning to respect.

"She's special. Don't hurt her or we'll kick your ass," Nick said and Luke nodded with him.

"Yeah, okay." Finn picked the dumbbells up, his signal that he was done talking. He almost sighed in relief when the brothers turned away and went back to work.

After the gym, he dropped by his sisters', praying that Jenna would be there so he could talk with her. He knocked on the door.

Jenna opened the door, saw him, and slammed it in his face.

He reached for the knob since he didn't hear her lock the door. It opened and he stepped through, only to have Jenna try to push him back out the door.

"I don't want to talk to you." She reached up to slap him and he caught her wrist.

"What the hell is your problem? I came to visit Kelsey." He let that sink in until her arm went limp.

"You're not here to lecture me?" Her green eyes watched him closely.

"No." He lied, stepping around her and shutting the door behind him. "I don't care what you do."

A flash of hurt surfaced in her eyes before she drowned it out with indifference. "Fine." She left him standing in the foyer, returning to the living room.

He followed her, saw Kelsey sitting on the couch with wide eyes. It seemed Jenna's behavior shocked her still. It didn't him, expecting Jenna to be wild and crazy kept him from going insane. "Hey, Kelsey. I wanted to drop by and see if you needed anything else done? I noticed the paint on the house needs a touch up."

"Thanks, Finn. That'd be nice." Kelsey nodded.

He could tell she knew what he was really here for. Kelsey didn't have to be here for this, but he knew she wouldn't leave him to deal with Jenna by himself.

Jenna plopped down next to Kelsey and took the drink from her hands to take a sip.

Finn shook his head, hating that his youngest sister was such a spoiled brat. He wasn't sure what happened to make her that way, as she was spoiled the same amount as the rest of them. She just saw what she wanted and took it, damn the consequences or the damage done to everyone else. Kelsey wouldn't stand up to her, preferring to just let her have her way.

He had to figure out how to talk to Jenna without getting her guard up. There really wasn't a way to do that so he just said, "I hear you're seeing a doctor now."

Jenna shot Kelsey a dark look. "You told him."

"No, she didn't," Finn said, protecting Kelsey, who shot him a grateful look. "We live in a small town where most of the people have known each other for most of their lives. Did you think I wouldn't find out?"

Her careless shrug ignited his temper. "Damn it, Jenna. He had a wife."

"So. He didn't love her."

He stopped walking, stared at her in disbelief. "Are you serious? He didn't love her, so it was okay to just ruin their marriage? How are you that damn stupid?"

"I'm not stupid!" Jenna shot off the couch. "He chose me."

Finn made himself stay where he was. Shaking her wouldn't get his point across. "He chose you? Do you think he's going to be faithful to you? You weren't the only one he slept with." He'd found that out by asking around. "The man is a womanizer, do you really think he's not going to sleep around on you?"

Tears welled up in Jenna's eyes. "He said he loves me. That I'm different, and that I'm all he needs to be happy. He's going to buy us a house and let me move in with him. He's going to marry me."

"Jesus, Jenna. Just..." Finn couldn't believe she believed the man. His sister may be spoiled but she wasn't normally that stupid. His hands fell to his sides and he cast Kelsey a confused look when Jenna ran out of the living room. A few seconds later, the door to her room slammed.

"She's lost it," Kelsey said.

Finn sank down onto the couch. "How can she really think that he'd change his ways?"

"I don't know. I've met him once, and he was a slimy pervert."

"Here?" Finn hated to think the bastard came into this house.

"No," she said, "it was at a restaurant. Jenna went to the bathroom and he hit on me the whole time. When I tried to warn her, she told me I was jealous and wanted him for myself."

Finn heard the undercurrent of pain in her voice. "I know you don't think you'll ever fall in love again, but Isaac wouldn't want you to be lonely for the rest of your life."

Kelsey sucked in a deep breath, nodding to keep the tears at bay. "I know. I just can't think of someone else right now. I miss him so much."

"I saw your painting of him the other day. It was amazing." Finn smiled at her, trying to get her to smile back. "I know he sees it and thinks so, too."

Kelsey's mouth quirked up. "He loved all of my paintings. When Mom and Dad wanted me to focus on something else, he was the one who convinced them that this was it for me. What I wanted to do for the rest of my life."

"Yeah, he talked about your paintings all the time, even showed off the drawings you sent him to everybody that had eyes. He even showed a camel once." Finn's chest constricted when he talked about his best friend, but seeing the love in Kelsey's eyes, the happiness at remembering Isaac, had him ignoring it. "He would want you to be happy, remember him with happy memories."

Kelsey nodded, her hands fiddling with the necklace Isaac had given her before he died.

"A friend invited me to go on vacation with them in Virginia Beach next weekend." He didn't know why he brought it up.

"That's nice." She watched his expression. "Why is that

not nice?"

Finn shrugged.

"Finn. What is it?"

"There's this girl," he saw Kelsey's eyes light up. "Not like that. She's annoying and stubborn. She's wild, like Mia was."

"That doesn't mean she's not a good person. Mia always reminded me of Jenna."

"She's not like that, but she does like having a good time. I met her in a bar." Finn pointed out.

"You were in the same bar, does that make you wild and crazy?" Kelsey countered.

"But I'm me."

Kelsey laughed at his reasoning. "And she's her. That doesn't mean she's like Mia, Finn. That just means that she doesn't mind going out and having a good time."

Finn's mouth twisted. "Maybe. But it doesn't matter, I'm not looking for anything right now."

Kelsey got up on her knees, her hands going to the sides of Finn's face. "Isaac wouldn't want you to live like this either. He'd want you to be happy and in love. Don't make yourself miserable because you think you should've died instead of him."

Chapter Thirteen

Addie

All her bags were packed and she was actually excited about going to Virginia Beach. Finn would be there and she wanted some one on one time to try and figure him out. After dropping off Harlow at Victoria's, she headed toward Gemma's. They were heading down there together in a rented SUV. The weather was perfect, a little hot but a good breeze kept Addie cool enough. She pulled in behind Gemma's car and saw the SUV parked on the street. Thank God it looked roomy enough to fit all of them without having to sit on top of each other.

Finn was putting his bags in the back of the SUV. Addie stopped for a minute, watching his movements. His hands moved deftly, confidently, and she suddenly wanted them on her body. For a second she forgot all the reason she didn't want to sleep with him and just *wanted* him.

He glanced over his shoulder, the dark green t-shirt

brightening the green in his eyes. "Want me to get those?"

Addie blinked, her fantasy evaporating. "No, I've got it." She started toward the SUV again. Finn ignored her protest and took the bags from her. Instead of fighting with him, she watched him lift her bags into the back, the bottom of his shirt sliding up to reveal his abs. A tattoo snaked up his left side and Addie wanted to know where it led in his pants.

Seeing him in just a pair of swimming shorts, walking out of the water and dripping wet, was going to make her ovaries explode. She just knew it.

"Addie, did you bring snacks?" Gemma walked out of the house carrying a cooler. "I've got drinks."

Addie held up the bag Finn didn't take. "Right here. Cheetos, Slim Jims, you name it. We'll be set for our drive."

"Good." Carter shut the door to Gemma's house and locked it.

It wasn't lost on Addie that he now had a key, but she didn't say anything. That was between them.

Finn shut the back of the SUV whenever he finished and stepped away from it. He wore a pair of khaki shorts with his t-shirt, flip flops, and sunglasses perched on the top of his head. Addie wondered how long the ride would seem with him in the backseat with her. She had no doubt the lovebirds would want to sit up front together.

"Let's get this going. Ride's going to be long anyway." Carter slid into the front seat and started the SUV.

Addie went around and got in the back. Once Gemma and Finn were in, Carter pulled away from the house. "Autumn and Caleb are coming up tomorrow. Autumn had something to do with her mom, and asked Caleb to ride with her so she wouldn't be alone."

Finn shifted in the seat and even though there was a space between them, it felt like he was right next to her. The car was suddenly too hot and small for Addie. With him less than a foot away, legs stretched out and an arm slung over the back of the seat, she found it hard to breathe. His fingers grazed the back of her neck before he snatched them away.

He shot her a glance she couldn't read before pulling his arm back. She thought she saw desire that mirrored her own flash in his eyes, but he looked out the window before she could be sure.

Carter soon got on the interstate and Addie mentally prepared herself for hours of torture. Normally she loved road trips, had all kinds of fun games or things to talk about, but Finn was throwing her mind and body into a frenzy. There was no way she could think straight while he was so close to her.

She took out her cell and texted Halle to see what was up. She didn't have to wait long for an answer.

Halle: Nothing, waiting on Nick and Victoria to get to Mom and Dad's.

Addie: They're not upset I'm not there?

Halle: No, and why are you texting me when you have a hot firefighter sitting next to you?

Addie stifled her laughter as she put the phone up. Halle wasn't going to help distract her from Finn, she was pushing her to him.

Finn glanced over at her laugh, brows furrowed. She winked at him and couldn't hold back a smile at his confusion. He looked adorable like that.

"My sister is already at the condo with her family," Carter told them. "Her husband will be grilling dinner by the time we get there. Steaks, vegetables, salad."

Addie's stomach rumbled at the thought of such good food waiting on them after their car ride. She'd only brought snacks and looked forward to a good meal. "I can't wait."

Carter laughed at her obvious eagerness to eat and Gemma turned to look at her. "You have to leave some for us, you know."

"Yeah, yeah. I will."

The further they drove, the more aware of Finn Addie became. He sat still, but she could sense the tension in his body, waited for him to say something. She loved the sound of his voice. It was her mission this weekend to bring the Finn out that gave her the kitten that night. There had to be a way to get to him that didn't bring out his asshole side. As she snuck glances at him, she thought about that night. Not just the mind blowing kiss, but how he'd acted. Unsure of himself, but sweet. She wanted to bring that side out this weekend and see if she could get him to have a good time. He looked like he could use one.

Maybe she could also figure out what made him so sad. That haunting look in his eyes when they first met kept going around in her mind. The way he'd brushed his fingers over that one tattoo.

He probably wouldn't tell her about it, and she really didn't need to know, did she? That would be going too deep, too *relationship* like. All she needed to do was make sure he enjoyed himself.

She snuck another glance at him and started when she met his intense eyes. His eyes darkened and the car shrunk around her. Her nipples hardened as his gaze traveled down, caressing her with just a look. She stared at his lips and thought about the kiss again. He'd woken in her a desire for more than okay sex. More than great sex. She had a feeling that going to bed with him would be almost too much for her to handle and wanted to see if she was right.

His gaze returned to hers and when his lips twitched, she had to hold back from jumping him in the backseat of her friend's rental car. A flash of heat went through her body and pooled in the place she wanted him most.

For once, Addie turned away from a man that wanted her, and stared out the window. She didn't know if playing with fire this time was worth it. Maybe the burn would scar her.

A few hours later Addie was happy when they stopped at a burger place off of the interstate to grab some lunch and stretch their legs. She breathed in air that didn't smell like Finn, didn't heat her blood, and walked around a bit before following the others inside.

Finn still didn't speak unless it was to order his food or if he and Carter were talking. Her pride stung a little that he wouldn't talk to her, not like the night they kissed, like he was purposefully putting her at arms length. Didn't he know that by doing that, he created a challenge for her?

That he was daring her to break through those walls he erected?

When they finished eating they piled in the SUV and started the rest of their ride. Addie joked around with Gemma and Carter, determined to have a good time even if Finn was aloof. It rained hard about thirty minutes before they arrived, so when they stepped out of the vehicle in the condo's driveway, the ground was soaked.

Addie stepped carefully so she wouldn't slip, and stretched her arms above her head. Gemma stood beside her and slipped an arm around her waist.

"We are going to have so much fun." Gemma laid her head against Addie's. "I was really nervous about meeting his sister by myself."

"She's going to love you." Addie whispered to her as a woman flew down the stairs and wrapped Carter in a hug. She had beautiful caramel skin and light brown eyes that eyed Gemma curiously.

"Gemma, this is my sister, Sasha." Carter moved to stand beside Gemma. "Gemma, Sasha."

Sasha smiled, showing perfect white teeth, and hooked an arm through Gemma's. "I'm anxious to get to know the girl that stole my brother's heart. And her friend." Sasha nodded Addie over and hooked her arm through hers.

"Leave the men to get the bags, we'll talk inside."

Addie grinned at Gemma. She didn't think Gemma was going to have a problem. When she glanced over her shoulder, Finn was watching her walk away, face expressionless.

The condo was two-story with hardwood floors and a charming living room. The kitchen was done in sky blue with white cabinets, and Addie knew Victoria would've loved to get her hands on this place. Through the glass doors that led to the back porch, Addie saw a tall man at the grill and a boy standing next to him. She guessed that was Sasha's husband and her son, Trent. From the looks of things, the dad was teaching the son to grill. Addie wondered if her dad sometimes wished he'd had a son to teach those things.

Now he had Nick, and by blood, Luke. He'd always liked the boys, and now Nick was practically his son-in-law.

"Sasha, this is Addie." Gemma interrupted her thoughts. "She teaches at the elementary school with me."

"It's nice to meet you." Sasha poured them each a glass of lemonade.

"Thank you for inviting us." Addie took the glass Sasha held out and sipped.

"I don't get to see Carter very much and he's talked about Gemma for a while, so it was easy to invite her. I thought she'd be more comfortable with some friends here, too, since meeting the boyfriend's family can be scary." Sasha smiled over at Gemma. "I haven't heard Carter talk about a girl like this before, and I love you already."

Gemma beamed. "He's an amazing man."

Addie resisted rolling her eyes. Gemma had fallen hard.

"Trent and Zach are grilling the steaks now, and I already made the veggie packs that they're doing, too. And the salad's made, so all you need to do is settle in. There's six rooms upstairs and you can pick whichever isn't taken."

They heard the front door open.

"I've got the bags." Carter called out. "We'll carry them upstairs and you can pick the rooms."

"Go ahead, pick a room." Sasha shooed them out of the kitchen.

Addie sent Gemma a subtle thumbs up before they reached Carter and Finn. She walked up the staircase first, Finn a step behind her. After looking in the first three rooms, one being the bunk room for the kids, she found one that faced the ocean.

"Is it cool if I claim this one?" She looked at the others over her shoulder.

"Cool with us," Carter spoke up.

"Awesome." She stepped into the coral and grey decorated room and instantly loved the vibe of it. She'd definitely be able to relax here for the weekend.

"Here's your stuff."

Goose bumps formed on the back of her neck at his husky tone. She turned and smiled at him. "Thanks." He stood among her bags, which now sat on the floor, and she quirked a brow at him.

"Yeah, okay." He ran a hand through his short blonde hair and his eyes raked over her again.

Then he left, leaving her wishing he'd stayed and wanting his hands on her.

Chapter Fourteen

Finn

He left Addie standing in her room, his hands shaking. What the hell was wrong with him? His self control was close to shattering and it was all because of the woman who'd stood before him a few moments ago. The way she moved, the way she smelled, battered at the walls he'd built. Jesus, the weekend wasn't such a good idea anymore.

He picked a room, set his stuff down, and went to the bathroom. Turning the faucet on, he splashed his face with ice cold water. What he really needed was an ice cold shower, but dinner was almost ready. His mother was big on manners, and he wouldn't make the others wait to eat because he couldn't handle himself.

He dried his face with the little towel on the counter beside the sink, then went back out of the room. Addie's door was closed, thank God, because he couldn't handle going in there again, so he passed it and headed down the stairs. All of the people here knew each other in one way or another, and even though he and Carter worked together, he still felt a little out of place.

That wasn't really the problem. He always felt out of place, like he hovered outside life, not quite joining in or belonging.

Until he looked at Addie. He didn't want to examine what that meant, but when he looked at her, his whole word came into sharp focus. That night at her apartment the pressure in his chest disappeared and he could breathe again.

She stood with Gemma and Carter's sister in the kitchen and they all held a glass of red wine. Her hair was down and she laughed freely. He loved that sound, loved the way it washed over him.

When she spotted him, her laugh died. He could only imagine what his face showed her.

"This is my friend, Finn." Carter pulled him into the kitchen. "Finn, this is my sister, Sasha."

"Nice to meet you." Finn nodded to her.

"You, too." Sasha smiled up at him. "Want a beer?"

"Sure." Finn forced himself not to shove his hands in his pockets.

"I'll get it." Addie set her wine down on the counter and

grabbed him a beer from the fridge.

His fingertips brushed hers as she gave him the beer and the electric shot went straight to his cock. Damn it, he was going to need that shower after dinner. By the heated look in Addie's eyes she'd been hit by the same shock.

Her lips lifted in a slight smile before she turned back to her friends and her wine glass. Finn watched her for a minute, wishing he could brush the hair off her neck and touch his lips to her skin. Run his tongue over the sensitive spot where her neck and shoulder met.

Jesus, he needed to get a hold of himself before it got embarrassing.

"We're going to eat on the deck, is that okay?" Sasha asked.

"That sounds great," Gemma answered. She picked up the giant bowl of salad and carried it out.

"Carter, grab the utensils. Finn, grab the napkins. Addie, you can go ahead and have a seat outside," Sasha told them.

Addie shot him an amused glance, the humor sparkling in her eyes. He could tell she didn't mind Sasha's bossiness, in fact it seemed that Addie liked Carter's sister.

He grabbed the napkins and followed them outside. The air was cooling off as the sun set over the horizon. The dark ocean waves gently caressed the sand. That and the sound of Addie's voice had his body relaxing in a way it hadn't in a long time. Not since--no, he wouldn't think of that right now. Just for tonight, he'd enjoy himself with no guilt. Kelsey was right, Isaac wouldn't want him to be miserable. And he'd be the first one to tell Finn to have a little fun with Addie.

They sat down at the table, Trent claiming the seat in between his mom and his uncle.

"I hope you like your steaks medium." Zach passed around the platter that held the thickest steaks Finn had ever seen. He took one and set it on his plate, along with an aluminum foil pack of squash, carrots, zucchini, and tomatoes. He passed on the salad for now since there was no more room on his plate.

With his first bite into the steak flavor burst into his mouth. He savored it, realizing that he was actually enjoying eating something instead of everything being fuel for his body and nothing else.

"This is amazing." Gemma took a bite. "I've never had steak that was cooked perfectly, except in restaurants in the city."

"I wanted to be a chef when I was younger," Zach answered.

"It shows." Addie dug into her food with a zest that Finn found refreshing. He hated it when girls picked at their food.

They continued their meal, laughing and joking. Finn could tell Sasha really liked Gemma, and was thankful for that. Carter was head over heels and he'd hate to watch the drama of family versus girlfriend unfold. He'd seen it happen too many times with Jenna.

After dinner Finn and Carter volunteered to do the dishes since Zach and Trent cooked. It didn't take long, and once they had the dishwasher loaded, Finn started it.

"Carter, let's take a walk on the beach." Gemma popped into the kitchen as soon as they were done.

"Sure, babe." He wrapped his arms around Gemma's waist and pulled her closer.

Finn instantly felt awkward watching them. He backed up and went out the side door onto the deck. Carter's family was going to see a movie that Trent was waiting to see, and he had no idea what Addie was doing.

He watched the ocean, feeling a weird sense of calm envelop him. He'd always loved the beach, loved swimming in the ocean, and hanging out with his friends.

A memory of Isaac hit him and almost brought him to his knees. A beach similar to this one, Isaac grinning as they played volleyball with his sister and friends. He placed his forearms on the wooden railing and rested his head in his hands. Oxygen seemed scarce, so he sucked in a few deep breaths.

"Finn." Addie's voice broke through the grief. She placed a hand on his shoulder, searing the skin underneath.

He soaked her in for a minute, the feel of her touch, before lifting his head. His agony shone in his eyes, but he didn't care. Sometimes it was so hard to fucking breathe with Isaac gone.

"Hey," she said softly, "let's take our own walk, okay?"

It was dangerous territory to be alone with her, but he wasn't going to say no. She held out her hand and he took it as she led him down the steps to the white sand. He didn't let go of her hand as they started walking in the opposite direction of Gemma and Carter, but she didn't seem to mind.

Moonlight glinted off of partly unearthed shells and the water lapping at the sand. A little of his grief subsided as they walked, the cold sand pushing between his toes. Addie's hair shifted in the light breeze, making him glance down at her. She was watching the waves, and flicked her eyes up to meet his.

The electricity that zinged through him at the look in

her eyes was like a punch to the gut. It was soft, gentle, but it was the understanding that knocked the breath out of him. He didn't feel like she would judge him for the way he felt, for the darkness that chased him at every turn.

"What haunts you, Finn?" Addie placed a hand against the stubble on his face.

The touch shot straight through him. He closed his eyes, savoring the feel of it.

"You don't have to tell me if you don't want to." She tugged the hand she held, pulling him into an easy walk over the sand again.

Did he want to tell her? Open all the wounds he'd forced shut? He was afraid of what would bleed out if he did.

"I need some more time," He whispered, afraid that she would get angry at his resistance to talk about it.

"Okay."

Just okay. No harsh sound to it, the smile stayed on her face. God, it was such a sweet smile. Relief washed over him and he stopped. She stilled beside him.

"Did I say something wrong?" She tilted her head up to see him clearly. The moonlight lit up her features and he thought she looked ethereal, his angel in the darkness. Maybe a fallen one, but an angel still.

"No." He stepped closer, his fingertips brushing her jaw line. "Not wrong at all." His head dipped lower and he brushed his lips over hers, softly at first, and then as the desire roared through him he angled his head and fully captured her lips. Her hands slid up his chest and circled his neck, fingertips sliding into his hair at the base of his skull.

He hardened instantly, he wanted her with a fierceness that surprised him. It had been so long since he'd actually *wanted* a woman like this, with this kind of reckless passion. A fire raced through his blood and he didn't want to extinguish it.

She melted into him, all soft curves. He put a hand on her hip, the other on the side of her neck. He loved the way she fit against him, perfectly, and he wanted to see what other ways they could fit together. When she bit his bottom lip, then stroked her tongue over it, his cock jumped. Yeah, he definitely wanted to see what other ways they fit.

He lifted his head, stared into her desire filled eyes. "Want to go back to the condo?"

"Hell yeah, I do." She took his hand, pulled him back to the condo.

They walked at a faster pace than they'd came and were at the house in a matter of minutes. He pulled her up the steps, through the back door, and up the stairs to her room.

As soon as he shut her bedroom door, he pushed her up against it.

He had to have his hands on her, all of her.

Chapter Fifteen

Addie

Holy shit, Finn was hot. Totally hot and he was kissing her, hard. It was a kind of hard she liked, although she could feel the desperation and sadness behind it, even if he didn't realize it was there. His lips pressed to the spot where her collarbone and neck met and her knees weakened. She grasped his shoulders, feeling the firmness of the muscles underneath shift as he picked her up. Her legs automatically went around his waist as he walked them to her bed, all without breaking the kiss.

She was no innocent when it came to sex, she'd lost her virginity a long time ago, but something about the way Finn made her feel, how nervous she was, made it feel like the first time all over again.

Her back met the mattress and she reached her hands for the bottom of his t-shirt. She pulled it up and off even as he nibbled on her earlobe. She gasped as he bit down, then laved it in slow, sure strokes. His hand moved, pushing her shirt up her body, his fingertips sparking little fires everywhere they brushed.

"Hmm." Finn leaned up on his forearms. His thumb brushed the underside of her breast through the lacy bra.

The husky tone of his voice sent heat spiraling into her abdomen and her panties dampened. Jesus, he was just so…male. She reached her hands between them to the button on his zipper. It took her a few tries, with Finn nuzzling the line of her bra across the swell of her chest, and she couldn't think straight. Her brain was only sending signals to one place. She fumbled it open, gently pulled the zipper down, being careful not to pinch his hard-on with it.

He moved off of her for a moment, shedding his jeans, standing there in a pair of black boxer briefs that hung low on his hips. His erection looked like it was barely contained in them, and she wanted him to take those off too. Apparently he saw the look in her eyes and sent her a lopsided grin.

When he came back to her he hooked his fingers in the waistband of her shorts and whipped them off. She had no idea where they went and she really didn't care. She wanted his weight on her, in her. As she was about to say this, he trailed a finger over the dampness of her panties, brushing her clit, and her mouth closed. Her gaze shot to his, his eyes dark and hungry. His intenseness would've scared her if she hadn't wanted him so much.

That focus, it unnerved her even as it excited her.

Slowly, so slowly he pulled her panties off, letting them slide down her legs. His eyes followed the movement. Addie's throat went dry with desire, her heart racing. A virgin, she felt like a fucking virgin. Like he was erasing every other man's touch, branding her as his own.

She shivered.

"Cold?" He asked.

She swallowed and shook her head slightly. She was afraid to move, caught in him. His fingertips trailed back up her legs, pushed them apart. For a glaring moment, Addie felt completely exposed in a way she never had before.

Until he whispered, "You are so beautiful."

He crawled back on the bed, leaning over her and kissed her. It was deep, and she loved the taste of him, the smell of him, the feel of him. She wanted to feel more, so much more.

When he asked her to lean up she did, and he unhooked her bra. The straps fell down her shoulders and then the bra was gone. His tongue swirled around a nipple and her fingers dug into his shoulders. She arched into him, his hardness hot on her thigh. If she could think straight, she'd get those briefs off of him, then they'd be even, equally exposed.

"Off. Take them off." Addie managed to get out between gasps. His lips teased one nipple, his hand the other. "Please."

He stopped, looked at her from under hooded eyes. "If you want me to."

She nodded, sure he could see how hard her heart beat in her chest. Was he just as affected by this as she was? Did he feel new at this? No, he was too damn confident. In the way he moved over her, teased her. She watched him discard the black briefs and her eyes rounded. Holy shit, he was so hot. Her gaze roamed over his body, liking the fitness he'd kept as a firefighter.

"Better?" He murmured when he lay beside her, hand on her hip.

She nodded, there was no way words were coming out. Her brain and heart had stuttered at the sight of him.

He rolled on top of her and she bit her lip as his cock pressed against her clit. He kissed her again like he was savoring her taste. She'd expected him to be fast and hard, not take his time. Not be this gentle. She wasn't sure what to do with him. He always surprised her.

She sank into the kiss, letting her thoughts go, focusing on him. The way he felt. The way he moved over her. When he broke the kiss he moved lower, teasing her nipples with his hand. He kept going until his warm breath teased her.

His tongue stroked out, running up her center, and she flinched from the acute punch of desire that tore through her. Her legs tensed and he chuckled. "You won't forget this, Addie."

She wasn't going to argue with him. "You talk too much."

His lips quirked before he lowered his head. Her body arched into his mouth, pressing as close as she could. His tongue stroked as he ran his hands down her hips, squeezing her thighs. He tightened his grip, holding her down and she gasped at the erotic feeling. There was no where for her to run or hide now. He saw her, the real her, and she wondered if it was a good thing.

Her eyes closed as the tension built, then exploded through her. He didn't stop, determined to wring every last breath out of her.

When he finally climbed back up her body and pressed the tip of his cock at her entrance, she tried to catch her breath. But just that swiftly he pressed into her, stretched her, and the breath left her body again.

"Oh." Addie, the one who always had something to say, was speechless. He moved, pushing in further, and her eyes slammed shut at the sensation. Every nerve ending pulsed in her body, giving her heart something to race with. She'd never felt so much, so intensely, as she did right now. Every millimeter he moved shot through her system.

His lips pressed to hers, softly, as he began to thrust. She wasn't sure what she'd expected, but this wasn't it. This was more than she ever realized, something she didn't know she needed. Her hands ran up his chest, a light sheen of sweat already coating their bodies. She didn't care, just wanted him closer. Her hand went to the nape of his neck and she pulled him closer, skin to skin, as he picked up his pace.

She moved with him and the sensations started. It didn't take long for the orgasm to overtake her.

"Jesus, Addie. Squeezing me so tight." Finn's breath was ragged against her shoulder.

She tumbled into another orgasm as he let go, pushing in and out with a reckless abandon, his teeth biting into her shoulder. The orgasm didn't stop, all the muscles in her body tightened. All she could do was let go with him, walk into the fire that burned so brightly between them.

Chapter Sixteen

Finn

What the fuck just happened? Finn stared down into deep blue eyes, and could feel himself falling into them. He was propped up on his elbows, still inside her, after the most mind-blowing sex he'd ever had. He didn't want to sound like a bitch, but he'd felt connected to her.

One of her hands was in his hair, the other on his chest. He was sure that his heart beat matched the racing of hers. He hoped like hell his emotions weren't showing on his face. Did he even know what those emotions were? All he'd felt for a long time was pain, anger, fear, and grief that eclipsed those. This woman had somehow snuck in and managed to soothe those raging emotions enough that he could think straight again.

He should've listened to himself when he said she was dangerous. Damn it.

"Thinking pretty hard there." Addie smirked at him.

Knowing that he was heavier than her by more than a hundred pounds, he reluctantly pulled out of her and propped up on his elbow beside her. His hand rested on her hip. "Just thinking you rocked my world."

"Charmer." Addie laughed quietly. "Who knew you could be something other than an asshole?"

He smiled and realized that it was getting easier to do that around her. "It's a crazy world."

She cocked her head to the side. "If it's awkward to stay and talk, you don't have to. I'm a big girl, I know that adults have one night stands."

His heart clenched. "Want to be rid of me so quickly?"

"Nope. Just giving you an out if you want one." She watched him silently and he knew she waited on an answer.

It was one of the reasons he liked her. She didn't put pressure on him, didn't expect him to stay. He guessed that's one of the reasons he decided to. "I'm good right here, if you don't mind."

She beamed at him and his heart stuttered. Holy Christ, she could blind someone with that. When she snuggled up to him he didn't feel his usual panic at being so close to someone else. Vulnerable and naked. He thought only of how she fit against him, and how beautiful she was. "Was it good for you?"

Her snarky tone startled a laugh out of him. She playfully punched his chest.

"Shh, Carter's sister might be back with the kid. He doesn't need to hear us in here together."

He lifted a brow. "Is that so? You're not afraid of being caught with me?"

"I haven't been afraid of that since I moved out of my parent's house." Her eyes sparkled with mischief.

"You were a trouble child, weren't you?" He drew random circles on her hip.

"All the time. I had to be the bad one, my sisters were so good. One of us had to keep our parents on their toes."

"They're very nice, your family," He told her.

"They are." She smiled up at him. "I was very lucky that way. What about yours?"

He didn't mind answering these types of questions, he could give surface answers without digging too deep. "You know I have four sisters. My parents are divorced but still friends."

She traced the tattoos on his forearm, the one that was drawing circles on her. His arm stilled as she traced the shield, the Celtic knot inside of it. Strength, warrior. He was supposed to be both, and failed at them.

"You're not allowed to frown after you've had sex with

me. That could be very damaging to my ego." She leaned up and kissed him.

When she pulled back, he was smiling. Her kiss had shoved the thoughts right out of his mind.

"I wouldn't want to dent your inflated ego." He dodged the punch that came at his arm, rolled on top of her, pinning her hands above her head. "Maybe I should pay special attention to you." He watched her breath catch as he used a hand to brush against her nipple. Already he wanted her again with a desperation that scared him.

§§

The next morning he woke in his own bed, alone. Would Addie's feelings be hurt that he hadn't stayed the night with her? He'd come a little way, able to actually enjoy himself, but he wasn't ready to sleep with someone next to him.

He scrubbed a hand over his face and sat up. Golden light filtered through the curtains, so he knew it was after dawn. Then it hit him. No nightmares haunted him last night. No screams, no blood, no death. Isaac's ghost had been silent.

Maybe he really should go to therapy. Just the thought

of going made him want to build up walls like the Great Wall of China, but he forced himself to actually consider that it might help him.

What was she doing to him? He was already rethinking things he'd been dead-set against for a long time.

Voices drifted up the stairs, and he listened for hers. She was talking with Gemma and Sasha, and he could hear some type of cartoon on the TV. He dressed quickly, pulling on a pair of shorts and a t-shirt, brushed his teeth and headed downstairs.

Addie glanced up when he entered the room and smiled. He took that as a good sign that she wasn't angry with him. He caught the look Gemma sent him when she noticed Addie's smile, but ignored it. His gaze swung back to Addie, who was making him a cup of coffee.

"Thanks," he said. Awkwardness began to settle over him, he didn't know what to do. Did he lean down and kiss her? Did she want to keep their night a secret? Women were too damn confusing.

"You've got that frown again." Addie watched him and he wondered if she could see right through him.

Sasha rescued him from just standing there and staring by saying, "There's scrambled eggs and bacon in the microwave. Carter and Zach went out for a run, so some of it's theirs."

Finn nodded and grabbed a paper plate off the counter. After getting some of the food, he took a seat at the table. Addie slid into the chair next to him and sipped out of her mug. Gemma and Sasha sat too, and he listened to the feminine conversation that floated around him. He was used to it.

"We can head down to the beach when the guys get back. Trent's wanting to swim in the ocean, try to wakeboard. We can pack some snacks and drinks, that way we won't have to keep coming up to the house for those," Sasha told them.

"I love the beach." Addie smiled over at Finn. "Don't you?"

He shrugged and she quirked a brow. Why did he feel so awkward right now? She didn't act like it was a big deal that they slept together. In fact, she acted like it hadn't affected her at all when it had seared into his memories. That hit his ego hard, knocked it down to its knees.

"Addie, let's go get our bikinis on." Gemma stood and nodded toward the stairs. "I need your opinion on which one to wear for the first time Carter sees me in one."

"He's already seen you naked, what's the difference?" Addie asked.

Gemma blushed and Sasha laughed, then said, "Don't be embarrassed. It's not like I have delusions that you two are in that room and not doing anything. This isn't the fifties."

Gemma shook her head, smiling a little. "Addie, I swear."

Finn watched them head to the stairs, wondering if Addie knew that it was different to see women in bikinis, the promise of what was under them an intriguing puzzle even if you'd seen them naked before. He was looking forward to seeing what she looked like in hers.

Chapter Seventeen

Addie

The sun shone brightly, the perfect day for sun bathing and enjoying the company around her. Sasha and Gemma were lying beside her on the large blanket they'd carried down and the guys were in an impromptu game of football. Every once in a while she'd lift her head to catch a glimpse of Finn in his swim shorts, bare chested, throwing the ball.

Just the sight of him heated her skin. She hoped that her hard nipples weren't visible in her bikini top. Trent noticing would be more than a little embarrassing. Hot air brushed over her already hot skin, and she reached for her water bottle.

"You were staring again." Gemma opened one eye as she said it. She was lying on her stomach, arms folded and her head resting on them. The white bikini with gold polka dots they'd finally picked looked great on her.

"Shut up." Addie grinned over at her as she sipped the

cold water. "I slept with him last night."

"You shut up." Now both of Gemma's eyes were open. She sat up a little. "No, don't shut up. Spill details."

Addie glanced over to make sure Trent was out of earshot. "It was amazing."

"He looks like it would be," Sasha put in. "I'm happily married and I noticed his hotness."

Addie grinned. "He's even hotter naked."

Gemma and Sasha stared at her and she knew they wanted more details. "He looks like he'd be rough, right? And that's what I expected, and then he goes and surprises me by being gentle and so," she searched for the right word, "romantic."

"Romantic?" Gemma propped herself up on an elbow. "You've never considered sex romantic."

Addie shrugged. "I know. It was different with him."

"Damn it. Are you in love with him?" Gemma asked.

"No." Addie laughed, but it was weak. Thinking about falling for someone caused her heart to misfire. "No, I was just saying."

Sasha and Gemma shared a look, but Addie pretended to ignore it. She leaned back and slid her sunglasses on, effectively cutting off the conversation. Now the moment was ruined, not by them, but by the questions in her mind.

She couldn't be in love, she'd sworn it would never happen. Not after watching her sisters' marriages crumble.

Sasha and Gemma talked over her, light conversation, and Addie listened. A little while later she flipped over on her stomach and watched the guys, who'd now moved to the water. Zach was standing next to Trent, who was trying to surf the small waves on the wakeboard. No matter how many times he fell, he didn't give up, and Zach didn't tire of the game.

Finn and Carter helped too, and her heart melted at that. They were both just as patient with Zach and it awakened something in her she didn't want to face. She pushed it down and dropped her head onto her forearms. Sweat trickled down her back and between her breasts, the sun still steadily beaming down. She didn't mind, though, knew it was going to be this hot.

They went inside for a late lunch of sandwiches and chips, then started showering. Addie went to the upstairs bathroom and quickly bathed so that the others could get clean, and went to her room wrapped in a towel. She shut her door behind her.

A hand reached over her shoulder, then spun her around. Her hands clutched the towel, but she was prepared to beat ass if she needed to. She relaxed for a second when

Finn's green eyes met hers. "Hey."

He didn't say anything. His eyes dipped down and she swore she felt the caress of the gaze on her breasts above the towel. With one hand he brushed hers aside and opened the towel. Addie was trapped in his gaze, and her breathing turned ragged. His other hand dove into her hair and he crushed his mouth to hers. She responded instantly, not realizing until that moment how bad she wanted this. Having him close, him touching her.

The towel dropped to the floor and she didn't care that she was naked or that the wood of the door was cold on her back. He was hot enough to make up for it. When he pulled away, she frowned.

"Do you know how hard it was to not drag you up here all day?" Finn pushed his shorts down and she saw he was already hard, his erection jutting up between them. The iron hard velvet skin pulsed against her stomach. He kissed her again, pressing her against him. He broke free of the kiss long enough to tell her to wrap a leg around his waist. "Fuck, you're already wet."

His words made her moan into his mouth. His cock pressed against that wetness and she whimpered. For not knowing that she wanted this, she was suddenly an addict. Her head leaned back, exposing her neck, as he slid inside her. This time his movements spoke of desperation that she also felt. He held her hips a bit away from the door so that his thrusts didn't push her into it.

Her hands went into his hair, holding on as he moved inside of her. There was no gentle Finn this time, this was more of what she'd expected, and it took everything she had to not cry out. She bit her lip, laid her head on his shoulder to muffle part of the cries she couldn't hold in. The house around her disappeared, he was all she saw. All she felt around her.

When his lips touched her neck and his tongue darted out, she shattered, tightening around his cock. He swore in a desperate whisper before he followed her, thrusting a few more times.

Addie held onto him, knowing that if she let him go, she'd become a puddle on the floor. He kissed her neck tenderly before sighing.

"I couldn't stand it anymore."

That was all he said, but the emotion behind it brought hot tears to her eyes. She wasn't a crier, never had been, but something in his voice sparked her own emotions. She bit down on her lip to stop the tears, then leaned back and looked at him. "It's okay, I was hoping last night wasn't an isolated event."

His crooked smile had her smiling in return. "You are addicting, Addie."

"I know." She winked at him. "Can you help me to the bed? I don't think I can walk right now." She giggled when he put her over his shoulder in traditional fireman style and dumped her on the bed. "Thanks."

He scooped up the towel by the door and passed it to her. She couldn't help but notice that this time the smile stayed on his face. It caused a weird sort of warmth in her chest, but she ignored it. No sense in getting freaked out over their weekend fling. "I need to shower before all the hot water is gone. Do you mind if I come back?"

"Did I mind a few minutes ago?"

"No." He bent down and pressed his lips to hers in a quick kiss before leaving the room.

"Damn it." Addie spoke to the empty room. She rubbed the spot in her chest where the warmth spread. "I don't need this complication. Sex is sex, not a relationship."

§§

The end of the weekend came too fast and Addie was actually sad to leave the beach house. She watched the trees and buildings speed by as they drove back, and she couldn't help but wonder what returning to Sanctuary Bay would do to the fragile bond between her and Finn. Was she ready to just brush this off as a weekend fling or did she want to admit that she wanted something more?

Gemma kept sending her surreptitious glances and Addie knew that not only would she have to explain what happened to her, but to her sisters. They would want to know.

Autumn and Carter ended up not making it due to a huge fight and Addie reminded herself to call Autumn when she got home. Autumn had a fiery personality to go along with her red hair, and she didn't take shit from anyone, especially guys. There was no telling what had sparked the fight and she wanted to find that out.

Her entire body hummed with need. Finn was in the backseat with her, by the driver's side door, but his large body had his knee brushing hers. Each time it happened, her breath caught in her chest. He seemed oblivious to her addiction, staring out the window, tapping his fingers on his thigh.

The music swam around them in the car, a beat pounding out of the speakers. She forced herself to stay put, she couldn't pounce on him in the car. Did he even want her to?

Cursing silently in her mind, she sighed. Within days he had her back in high school, wondering if he "liked her or not" and she didn't particularly enjoy it. Normally she had the upper hand, deciding whether or not she wanted to keep seeing a guy, and she usually decided not to. Those men had bored her, always the same, never surprising her.

Maybe it would be a good thing if they didn't see each other again. At the thought, her traitorous body cringed. To keep seeing a guy opened up the possibility of the relationship developing into more, and she didn't want that. She wasn't even sure why she'd suddenly decided that she wanted to have sex with him, there'd been something in his eyes, that haunting look, that had made the decision for her. He'd needed her, and without knowing it, she'd needed him.

Fuck, she was screwed.

Chapter Eighteen

Finn

Walking into his sisters' house, he called out for Kelsey or Jenna. When Jenna answered, he hoped that she wasn't still mad at him. He hated the way she lived her life, but he still loved her, and didn't like it when she was angry with him.

He entered the kitchen to see her and a guy sitting at the table. The guy was in a suit, minus the jacket, top button undone. He was blonde, with manicured hands, and a sleazy grin. Finn guessed this was the famous cheating husband that supposedly loved Jenna.

"Finn." Jenna squealed and got up to hug him. His arms went around her, all the while he watched the guy. Jenna pulled back and smiled at him. "I want you to meet Trevor."

Finn looked at the guy, didn't move to shake his hand when Trevor held his out. Trevor dropped his hand slowly, a fake smile spreading across his face. Finn hated men like this with a fierceness. They were slick liars who cheated on women.

Jenna smacked Finn's arm. "Is that any way to treat my fiancé?"

Jesus Christ, her fiancé? Finn frowned and finally noticed the diamond sparkling on her finger. His stomach churned. Didn't she realize this man was playing her? Even if he married her, it didn't mean he was going to be faithful. "Fiancé?"

Jenna nodded and clapped her hands together. "Isn't it amazing? We're going for a winter wedding, all snow and fairy tale lights. Right, baby?" She slid onto his lap.

Trevor smiled, showing too much teeth that reminded Finn of a shark. He ignored the smile and shoved his hands in his pockets. What the fuck? "Does Kelsey know?"

"I haven't had a chance to tell her yet. She's still at work." Jenna sighed and glanced back up at Finn. "Are you going to stay for dinner? Trevor's going to cook steaks."

No way in hell was he staying to watch this fiasco. "I just got back. I need to go by the station and check on things there." Finn backed out of the kitchen and reached for his phone. He was going to give Kelsey a heads up about Jenna. Once inside the car, he looked at the cell's display. He had a text from an unknown number.

UN: Miss me, Finn? Things are heating up, try not to get burned tonight.

What the fuck? Finn stared at the phone for a minute more. Maybe it was time to talk to the chief, find out what was going on. This was bordering on stalk-ish behavior.

When he pulled up to the station, Caleb was pushing a lawn mower over the grass and a few of the other guys were weed-eating and picking up sticks. "Need any help?" Finn called out to Caleb.

Caleb stopped the lawn mower and wiped his forehead with his arm. "Nah. We're almost finished."

There was an edge to his voice, and Finn guessed it was from the fight with Autumn. He'd heard Gemma and Addie discussing it in the car on the way back, when he wasn't completely consumed with keeping his hands off of Addie.

Caleb went back to mowing, muttering under his breath, as Finn walked inside the garage bay. The fire trucks shone in the lights so Finn knew someone had already washed them. Must've been one of the rookies.

Chief waved. "Want to take a shift tonight? Aaron has some stomach bug and I don't want him spreading it around."

"Sure." Finn didn't really have anywhere else to be. He

definitely didn't want to go to his sisters' house.

"Great." Chief nodded toward the sink of dishes. "That was his job. I've got some paperwork to finish that's due tonight." He disappeared back into his office.

Finn would have to talk to him later. He shook his head, but smiled, and walked to the sink. People thought fighting fires was glamorous and fun, but didn't realize they did so much more than that. Paperwork, marketing, helping in the community. Many of the bigger cities did things differently, not getting cats out of trees kind of thing, but in a town this small, you couldn't really tell the citizens no.

When he finished putting the dishes in the dishwasher, he turned it on. Caleb and the others were finished in the yard and showering up, so he figured he'd cook some spaghetti for all of them. Carter was still technically on vacation, and Nate and Noah were off tonight, and he realized he missed their crude jokes and humor.

Sleeping with Addie had made him a little girl, hadn't it? Finn browned the meat and tried to keep his mind off of Addie. He'd heard she was a one-night stand, or weekend, girl so he didn't have high hopes that the experience would repeat itself.

The fire siren blared out of the speakers, and Finn jumped. He'd been so deep in thought. He quickly recovered, turned the stove off, ran to get his gear on. Caleb flew by him, still dripping wet from the shower. Everyone threw their gear on and hopped into the truck. Chief sat in the driver's seat.

"It's the community center. There may be volunteers stuck inside, we're not sure how many. The center's normally closed on Sunday afternoons, and the volunteers clean and get stuff ready." Chief filled them in.

The sun was setting in the distance. Finn could see the reddish orange glow of firelight and black smoke rising against the horizon. Adrenaline flooded through his veins, and he felt alive, the numbness that sometimes haunted him evaporated like the smoke from the fire.

Chief parked the fire truck and they hopped out, putting on air-masks and pairing up. "Finn, Caleb-in the building. Check to see if there are survivors."

Finn hustled toward the building, hearing the Chief assign other tasks to the rest of the firemen. Within seconds the Chief's voice was drowned out by the roar of the fire, the crackle and groan of wood. Flames danced across the ceiling and along the walls as they stepped through the doorway. Even through his gear, he felt the heat press against him. Acrid smoke blew around them, making visibility close to zero.

Caleb tapped him on the shoulder, drawing his attention to the right. That was where the main room was, where Chief said the volunteers were most likely to be. Finn heard nothing but the fire around him and he hoped that was only because it was so loud, not because the volunteers were already dead.

He stayed close behind Caleb, dodging falling pieces of the ceiling. This fire was hot, very hot, and a trickle of unease ran down his spine. How had the fire gotten this hot so quickly? Something was wrong, he could feel it and it had something to do with the text the anonymous bastard sent him. The main room of the center was engulfed in flames, and they could tell this room was the point of origin but the arson investigators would decide for sure.

With decreased visibility, Finn felt along the wall and floor, holding his breath to listen for sounds other than the fire. Someone screaming, ragged breathing, painful moans and groans.

There. He turned his head to the left and strained to hear. There it was again, a moan. Moving slowly, he headed in that direction. Every few steps he stopped and listened to make sure he was still moving in the right direction. The toe of his boot hit something--or someone-- and he immediately crouched down.

What the fuck? Finn reached out and assessed the woman's body. She was naked, blood running down her stomach. Anger coursed through his veins to rival the heat of the fire. This hadn't been an accident, someone had hurt this woman, possibly the other woman with her, and set this fire to either cover it up or finish the job.

Carefully he put an arm under her neck and the other under her knees. Her eyelids fluttered but didn't open. Finn didn't like the ragged sound of her breathing, knew that the smoke inhalation might kill her. He moved back in the direction of the door, almost ran into Caleb.

"What the hell is this?" Caleb shook his head. He held another naked woman in his arms, blood running down her side.

"Don't know," Finn said as they moved toward the entrance.

Paramedics met them a few feet from the door and took the women to stretchers near the ambulances. Finn grit his teeth, his mind reeling. This was a small town, murder didn't just happen. He'd checked when his sisters moved here, Sanctuary Bay was supposed to have one of the lowest crime rates. Something about the pattern the blood on the women made teased at his mind, but he ignored it to start fighting the fire.

Chapter Nineteen

Addie

Sunday nights always irritated her. It meant the weekend was over, but more than that this time. Her weekend with Finn was over. She didn't know how he'd felt about what happened between them, he'd kept that hidden well.

"Addie, hellooo?" Autumn snapped her fingers in front of Addie's face.

Addie blinked, then gave Autumn a smile of apology. "Sorry, spaced out for a sec. What were you saying?"

Gemma rolled her eyes. "Addie's probably rehashing her sexy weekend with Finn."

Autumn's brow rose. "Oh? Here I am fighting with Caleb and you two get to have fun, sexy weekends? Not fair." Her smile took the sting out of the words. She sipped her rum and Coke. "I don't even know what we were arguing about, but I wasn't driving hours in a car with him.

Talk about awkward."

"I thought you didn't want to see him anymore," Gemma pointed out.

"He wanted to take me to dinner, I didn't want to say no to free food and a good time." She shook her head when both girls laughed. "Free food is a good thing."

"You sure it wasn't because you wanted a piece of him again?" Addie smirked. "I think you're hooked on him."

"What about you and Finn?" Autumn fired back, teasing Addie.

What about her and Finn? Addie didn't want to consider how bad she wanted to have him over tonight. Technically it was still the weekend, right? She could count it as a weekend fling. Tomorrow she could really start distancing herself from him.

"There she goes again." Gemma waved her hand in front of Addie's face. "Addie."

Addie sighed. "It was amazing. Not what I was expecting at all."

"A guy surprised you? You, who usually gets so bored with them after one or two nights?" Autumn leaned on the counter, eyeing Addie. "Intriguing. Could he be The One?"

"Shut up." Addie couldn't help but smile at Autumn's sarcasm. "No one's speaking of The One." She waved a hand in the air. "So, are you and Caleb for real over or what?"

"Nice deflection." Gemma looked to Autumn, "Are you?"

"I think so. He called me too complicated. Said he was looking for something simpler, that a relationship with me would be too confusing."

"Did you junk punch him?" Addie asked. "You should've junk punched him. All women are complicated, and he should know that."

"I think it's because I wouldn't agree to meet his parents."

"Parents? He's already throwing that into the mix? What does he expect from only a few weeks?" Gemma scratched Harlow behind the ears when she rubbed against her ankle.

"It's your fault, you know. You went to meet Carter's sister and that gave Caleb the idea." Autumn frowned. "But you and Caleb are different. Made for each other."

"Thanks." Gemma beamed at her. "I feel that way, too."

"Rub it in." Addie laughed. "You and your perfect man."

"You're damn right." Gemma swallowed the rest of her wine and looked at her watch. "I've got to get home and unpack."

"Yeah, I've got to do some laundry before tomorrow. I haven't done it in like a week. This was literally all I had to wear." Autumn gestured to her yoga pants and holey t-shirt.

"Nothing wrong with yoga pants." Addie called as they left. She sat in the silence for a minute, going over the weekend in her mind. After Friday night, she hadn't been able to keep her hands off of Finn every time they were alone. Never had she craved a man like that, having to feel his lips on hers, his hands running over her body. It's like she was born again into the sex life.

It didn't mean anything though. She'd push those cravings down, deep down underneath so they wouldn't surface again. Getting stuck in a relationship was not something she wanted to do. Ever. She preferred to be free to do what she wanted, when she wanted. No man was going to ruin her life like men had ruined her sisters'. No way was she going to go through that. Watching her sisters' lives crumble around them, the heartbreak that devastated them, had made up Addie's mind.

No relationships. That's why she avoided them like low-fat food. Neither interested her.

§§

Just as she was about to order Chinese, someone knocked on her apartment door. She looked at Harlow, who sat at her feet. "Who could that be?"

Harlow blinked at her sleepily. She smiled to herself and went to open the door. Her heart skipped a beat when she saw Finn standing there, in jeans and a t-shirt, but covered in ash and soot, smelling of acrid smoke. His eyes were solemn and she saw the anguish in them and the shadows under his eyes.

"Come in." She stepped back, let him in--in more ways than one. He carried a bag in his hand and stood in the entry way, looking lost. "Why don't you take a shower?"

He nodded and she took his hand, pulling him toward her bathroom.

"I only have girly smelling stuff." She brought out a towel and washcloth from the little closet. She waited for him to start pulling off clothes before going back into the living room. When she picked up Harlow--wanting to snuggle with something--she noticed her hands shook. Seeing him like that, lost and forlorn, had affected her much more than she thought it would.

Within fifteen minutes he appeared at the end of the hallway, looking into the living room, in a different pair of jeans and white t-shirt. She stood from the couch and moved to stand beside him. He watched her, face intense, and she saw the tension in his body. Like he was holding himself back from something.

"Finn." She whispered his name as she put her hands on his forearms where they were crossed over his chest. "Finn," she repeated.

"They're dead." His voice cracked and her heart plummeted.

"Who is dead?" Her mind raced, immediately thinking of her family, then his sisters, or Gemma and Autumn.

"The women from the fire. They died." He swallowed.

She had no idea what he was talking about, but pulled him to her room anyway. He was pale and it scared her, she wanted him to lie down. With robotic movements he stretched out on her bed, and she laid down next to him, both on their sides facing each other. His eyes were squeezed shut and his lips were in a hard line. Addie wanted to stroke a hand over his face, but was afraid of what that caring gesture meant.

"There was a fire at the community center earlier," he began, and Addie's heart started racing again. Sanctuary Bay was a small town, she'd most likely know who the two women were. "It was a large fire, and it took us forever to get it out. Caleb and I found the women in the main room." His breath shuddered and Addie prepared herself for whatever came next. "They had my tattoo carved into their stomachs. Somehow this is my fault, and I don't know why."

Addie tried not to think of the implications of that. "Which tattoo?"

"This one." He pointed to the tattoo she'd asked about the first night she met him. "My best friend, Isaac, talked me into getting it. He died in Afghanistan."

"God, Finn." Addie brought her hands up to his face this time, pressed a soft kiss to his lips. She wanted to erase the pain off his face, even if it was in the only way she knew how. She deepened the kiss, stroking her tongue over his lips and pulled him under with her.

Chapter Twenty

Finn

Dusk was beginning to brighten the room around him and he shifted in the bed. Addie was curled next to him, a leg slung over his. He didn't feel as claustrophobic as he thought he would, sleeping next to someone. Didn't feel as if some unknown enemy was going to kill him in his sleep. Maybe he was growing out of the feeling, or maybe it was because it was Addie lying next to him.

He'd had a new version of nightmares, the two women beseeching him as a dark shadow carved his tattoo in their stomach, fire and smoke twisting around them. The arsonist had hit close to home, and with that and the tattoo, it had to be someone he knew. Or maybe someone that knew of him. Whoever it was liked to taunt him with calls and texts. He turned it over and over in his mind, and he suddenly wondered if the beach house fire a few weeks ago had anything to do with this. He needed to talk to Chief and find out.

If it did have something to do with this, what would he do? It's not like he was a detective, although he could investigate if he needed. If it was someone who had a grudge against him, were his sisters in trouble? Was Addie? His fingers brushed the dark hair that touched his arm.

Relationships were complicated, even with what he and Addie shared. Not really a relationship, not really friends.

Addie stirred, running a hand up his chest. His thoughts instantly scattered and then focused on her warm body against his. "You have got to stop frowning." She pushed up on an elbow and kissed his jaw. "You were murmuring in your sleep. Nightmares?"

He sat up, an ice cold shiver running through him, shattering all thoughts of sex. People knowing about his nightmares was a weakness. They could use it to hurt him. Addie would look at him with pity, maybe even revulsion, if she knew. "No." His answer was curt and cold.

Addie sat up, too, cocking her head to the side. The fire in her eyes burned him, along with the quick flash of hurt. "What the hell?"

"It's nothing." He stood and shoved his jeans on. Not looking her in the eyes, he pulled his shirt and boots on. "I've got to go."

"Fine." Addie brushed her hair off her shoulder and he almost gave in to the desire to stay. She was a beautiful mess that he wanted to fall into.

Finn didn't look back as he left. Spending the night had shaken him, finding those women even more so. Addie's angry stare burned into his back but he ignored it, forced himself to forget it, as he climbed into his truck. He needed to speak with the Chief, needed to see the pictures from that first beach house fire. Something teased the back of his mind, an instinct honed from his time in war, and he knew something wasn't right.

When he pulled into the fire station, he saw the Chief's red pick-up truck. Good, he wouldn't have to have this conversation over the phone. It would make this already horrible situation a little easier.

"Hey, Finn." Aaron's red hair stuck up all over the place like he'd just woken up. "Heard about the fire last night. Hate I missed it."

"Yeah." Finn brushed by Aaron, telling himself he'd apologize for it later. Aaron didn't know he was in a hurry and was just trying to be friendly.

He found the Chief in his office, on the phone. Chief held up a finger and Finn sat in the chair across from his desk.

After a few minutes, Chief hung up. "The mayor."

Finn nodded, tapping his fingers on the wooden arm of the chair.

"What's on your mind? You shot out of here last night before I could talk to you. Are you doing okay after finding the two women?" Chief leaned forward, eyes intent.

"That's what I wanted to talk to you about." Finn sighed, decided that just getting it over with would be better. "Those women had my tattoo carved into their stomachs."

Chief slowly sat back, steepled his fingers. His brows furrowed as he watched Finn closely. "I know you didn't murder them. You were riding back with Carter and two women."

"Thanks for the vote of confidence." Finn ran a hand through his hair. "I don't know why that happened or what's going on, but I'd like to look through the photos from the beach house fire a few weeks ago."

"Do you think it's connected?" Chief asked.

"I've got a feeling they are, but like I said, I have no idea why. No one comes to mind, no one jumps out at me." Finn sighed. "Do you still have the photos here?"

Chief opened a drawer, pulled out a manila file. He held onto it for a moment before passing it to Finn. "These are everything the arson investigators had on it. If you see a connection to the fire last night, they need to know. The police are already involved. You'll need to give them a statement."

Finn nodded and opened the file. Pictures of burnt furniture, ashes, and walls assaulted him. It wasn't until the middle of the pictures that the chill ran down his spine and the hairs on the back of his neck stood up. "Shit."

"Did you find something?"

"Yeah." Finn took the picture out, laid it on the Chief's desk. It was a picture of the living room. It was faint, but carved into the coffee table was his tattoo. "It was easy to miss, because it's so faint. You had to know what you were looking for."

Chief looked at him. "And you don't have any idea who would want to do this?"

"No, but I've been getting hang-up calls, once the person threatened me, and a text before the fire that said things were going to heat up."

"Shit," Chief echoed. "When you give your statement, make sure you mention that."

Finn nodded and left the office, and since it was his day off, he thought he'd drop by the gym, do a little boxing, and maybe while he was doing that his brain would connect the dots. Addie kept popping up in his mind as he drove to the gym. He felt terrible for how he'd treated her, but it wasn't safe for her to be close to him. Not when he couldn't control his nightmares. He didn't want to hurt her.

After he went inside the gym, he changed his clothes in the locker room, locked up his wallet and casual clothes, and found an empty punching bag. Some of the guys were in the ring, but he wasn't in a mood to take it easy on someone. If he entered that ring, the other guy might not exit it breathing.

The punches felt good, like he was doing something--anything--even if it was stationary. He had to clear his mind, figure out what the hell was going on before more people were hurt, or worse, murdered. Black despair squeezed him when he thought about the women dying because someone had a grudge against him. But who could it be? He'd left the military behind and his friends had been sad to see him go. It had to be someone from the military though, because that's the only place his tattoo had been prominent, along with Isaac's. Was someone other than himself blaming him for Isaac's death? For the other members of the unit that had died that day?

Later today he'd have to get in touch with his old buddies, see if they've heard anything, whispers, angry comments.

Finn stayed at the gym until he couldn't see from the sweat that poured down his face and his shirt and shorts were soaked. He'd burnt off most of the frustration, but some of it still hummed underneath his skin. It only got worse every time Addie drifted into his thoughts. The look in her eyes when he'd brushed off her concern this morning pierced him every time he recalled it. He just didn't know what he'd do about it.

Chapter Twenty-One

Addie

How was she supposed to just roll over and forget Finn, even if he was being such an asshole? She saw the agony and despair in his eyes and body whenever she'd asked him about the nightmares he was obviously having. She had a feeling that he wasn't reacting that way to hurt her, but as some misguided way to protect her, or even himself. It wasn't like she couldn't understand the need to build walls. Hell, she had plenty of them herself.

She shut her car door and walked up the sidewalk to Victoria's. She was babysitting her nieces so that Victoria and Nick could have a date night. They were just going to dinner, so she'd get back at her apartment to feed Harlow on time.

"Hey!" Lucia opened the door. She was smiling again, and Addie couldn't help but wonder if Lucia had taken her advice about not sleeping with her boyfriend.

Feeling like she was betraying her sister by not saying anything, Addie stepped into the house and shut the door behind her. She needed to figure out when she and Halle could tell Victoria together. So far they'd procrastinated with it. "Hey. Ready for some movies? I stopped by the Redbox before I came."

"Sure." Lucia grabbed Addie's hand and led her into the living room.

Victoria came in, putting her earrings in. "Thanks for coming."

"You look great." Addie nodded at Victoria's grey dress. "It flatters your shape."

Her sister beamed. "Thanks for that, too. We should be back in two hours."

"We'll be fine. I'll make sure the girls go to bed on time." And make sure she talked to Lucia about the boyfriend situation. Maybe that would help her guilt lessen a little at not telling her sister about it.

Nick walked out of the kitchen, wearing upscale jeans and a button down blue shirt. It looked good on him, brought out the blue in his eyes. Addie was glad that her sister found someone who truly cared about her. "Hey, Addie."

"Hey." She waved them out the door. "We're going to

watch chick flicks and eat ice cream before they have to be in bed."

When the door shut behind them and Addie locked it, she went back into the living room. Helena was on the couch, Kindle in hand. "You planning on watching the movie with us?"

Helena blinked up at Addie, eyes finally focusing. "What?"

"The movie," Addie laughed, "are you going to watch it?"

"What is it?" Helena set her Kindle down on the armrest.

"The Proposal." Addie popped the DVD in the player. "Lucia, make the ice cream while I get it started."

"On it." Lucia disappeared into the kitchen and Addie heard her getting the bowls down.

"How's school going?" Addie sat beside Helena. She figured Helena wasn't having the same issues as Lucia, but last year Helena was bullied a lot. She wanted to make sure everything was okay with her, too.

"Good." Helena pulled her dark hair into a pony-tail. "No more bullying, if that's what you're worried about."

"You were always too smart for me." Addie hugged her close. She wanted what was best for them, for the girls to have a full and happy life. She worried about what effect their dead beat dad had on them. At least Nick had stepped up to the plate and was great with them.

Lucia returned from the kitchen with the ice cream bowls and passed them out. Once she was on the couch with them, Addie turned The Proposal on. It was one of her and the girls' favorites, so she knew it was a good pick for tonight. Addie was hoping that the movie would take her mind off of Finn for a little bit. She wasn't sure that was even possible.

She watched Ryan Reynolds and Sandra Bullock's amazing chemistry on the TV and wondered, did she and Finn have that chemistry? They sniped at each other enough, and there was fire in the bedroom. So yeah, they had that chemistry, but not the desire to commit to a relationship or anything more than a few flings. Doubts began to creep into the back of her mind, but she shoved them down, deep down, not wanting to examine them. What he'd said about the women dying, about his tattoo being carved into their stomachs, freaked her out. She knew he didn't do it, but who had a grudge against him that full of hatred? Who wanted to hurt him by hurting other women? By killing them and burning a building to the ground?

His past was mostly a mystery to her, as were his family and friends other than the guys on the fire department. What did she really know about him, other than the fact that two of his sisters lived here? She knew he was in the military once, and his best friend had died overseas, but that was literally all she knew about him. Addie was a private person by nature, so she understood the reasoning, the need to keep certain parts of yourself away from other people. God knows she didn't share her life with the men she normally slept with.

This thing with Finn was something different. She wasn't sure how to classify it, exactly.

"Are you going to eat your ice cream?" Lucia nudged Addie's shoulder.

Addie glanced down at the bowl of uneaten ice cream. It was her favorite, Triple Chocolate, so she should've finished the bowl off by now. She picked up the spoon and took a bite so the girls wouldn't worry about her. "I was distracted by Mr. Reynolds."

The girls laughed. By the time the second movie, Ever After, was over, Nick and Victoria returned. Nick stayed the night most nights, although he hadn't officially moved in yet.

"Thanks, Addie." Victoria's face was flushed.

Addie winked at her. "Enjoy yourself?" When Victoria laughed, Addie smiled. "Good. We watched the movies, the girls were good of course. I'm going to get home so I can feed Harlow."

"Okay. Be careful," Victoria told her.

As she headed home, Addie knew Victoria worried about her family driving after the wreck involving Helena at the beginning of the summer. Victoria was a little bit more paranoid now, but Addie took it in stride. She understood why it was that she did that. Once home, she fed Harlow, who meowed incessantly as soon as she walked inside the apartment. After that, she changed into yoga pants and a t-shirt and wondered what to eat. It's not like she was going to cook or anything. There were some frozen dinners in the freezer, so she decided on that. Simple and easy, with no dishes to clean up afterward.

Harlow snuggled up in the bed with her, and while Addie loved her snuggling companion, she kind of wished that Finn was there. Wished he was in the bed with her. Not just for sex, but to talk to. To laugh with. She wasn't sure what was coming over her but she knew she didn't like it.

§ §

The kids in her third grade class were insane the next day. Addie sat behind her desk, listening to them giggle and whisper before telling them to be quiet for the third time. She was already aggravated since she hadn't heard from Finn, but she'd be damned if she was going to contact him after his rebuff yesterday morning.

She finally stood and held up a hand. By the serious expression on her face, the kids quieted down. It was near the end of the day and she knew they wanted to leave, but they still had one more test to take. "Okay, kids. It's time for your spelling test. We have to get this done before you leave. It won't take long. If I see any cell phones out, you'll receive a zero on the test," she reminded them.

Several of the students groaned before putting up their phones.

She had them write their names on the paper—if there was ever something that truly frustrated her, it was getting a nameless test back—and then had them number it down. As she called each word out, she waited a few moments before calling out the next one. A few of the kids rushed and sat impatiently while she waited on the ones who were more careful. Each kid had a different learning style, different way of doing things and she loved learning how to make their minds and hearts grow.

When the test was finished, she gathered up their papers just in time for the end-of-the-day bell. Chaos erupted as kids jumped up with their bags in hand, yelling 'bye' to her as they ran out of the classroom. She took a deep breath and exhaled as she sat behind her desk, ready to grade the papers.

Chapter Twenty-Two

Finn

He met the detective outside of the station. Detective Krakowski was a little older than him, with sharp brown eyes and thick brown hair. "Thanks for meeting me."

"No problem. The chief told me you had a connection, your tattoo, to the fires? And that you were getting harassing phone calls and texts?" Krakowski brought out a little notepad and a pen.

"Yeah. It started a few weeks ago, but I brushed it off. At first I thought someone had the wrong number, but the second time they called they spoke. The voice was raspy, like they used a voice modifier. I can show you the texts." Finn pulled up the unknown number's text.

Krakowski's eyes narrowed on the screen. "Seems like someone has a grudge against you."

Finn repeated what he'd told the Chief about leaving the Marines on good terms. "I can't think of anyone off hand that would hate me this much."

"Someone does, but it doesn't mean that you know them. In a stalker's messed up mind, you don't have to actually speak with them to form that fascination." Krakowski closed the notepad. "I have your number. I can do a little digging, see what I come up with. Don't leave town."

Finn nodded. It wasn't like he had plans to leave Sanctuary Bay. Not now. He did have something to do, so he headed toward the elementary school.

He stared through the little window in the door, watching Addie as she sat behind her desk. Kids rushed down the halls behind him, eager to be home. He was eager to talk to Addie, to apologize for being such an ass. He'd wanted to apologize in person, because she deserved it. Sending a text would've been too cowardly.

He knocked gently on the door, a part of him hoping she didn't hear him so he'd have an excuse to leave, but she called for him to come in without looking up. He walked in, shutting the door softly behind him. She wore a dress that covered her cleavage and went to her knees, but his imagination filled in what was underneath. Shaking his head, he forced himself to focus. He'd come here to apologize, not jump her.

"Finn?" She'd finally looked up at him. "What are you doing here? Did you text me?"

"No," he said before she could look for her phone. "I wanted to talk to you in person."

"Oh." Her brows rose as she sat back in the chair. Her hair was up in a pony-tail, showing off her shoulders and neck. He wanted to press a kiss there, badly.

"I wanted to apologize for the other morning. I acted like a jerk, all because you were being nice to me, and I'm sorry." He sat on the edge of the desk.

"Okay." She shrugged. "You were under a lot of stress, and I was pushing. Have you found out anything about the fire and your tattoo? Or the creepy stalker calls?"

Her change of subject left him reeling for a second. "Um, only that the beach house fire from a few weeks ago was connected. No one was hurt but my tattoo was carved into the coffee table of the house."

"Finn, that's horrible." Addie stood and came around the desk.

"I know. I just don't know what to do about it. Or who is behind it." Some of the tension in his body dissolved when she wrapped her arms around his waist.

"You'll figure it out." Her voice rang with belief in him.

"How do you know that?" Finn pulled back to look at

her. "You've only known me for a month or two, and we've barely spoken about things that really matter."

"You could change that." She stepped away from him.

He resisted reaching out for her, then stopped. Why was he resisting the way she made him feel? "Addie, come here." He took her hand and he pulled her back to him. "You're right. We can both change that."

"True." Her lips lifted in a smile. "I hold back, too. I'm bad about it. I do it to keep from getting hurt, to keep people from getting close, other than my family. I have a feeling you do the same thing. I'm not asking you to spill your guts and tell me every dirty detail about you, but I would like to eventually know the things that matter."

Finn ran a hand up and down her back. "I'll try to do that. Try to share those things with you, eventually. I'm just not ready."

"I can handle that. But don't run off from me just because I ask you a question. You should be able tell by now that if you don't want to talk about something, I'll drop it. I won't nag you until you tell me." She moved to grab her purse. "Are you coming to my place or do you have somewhere you need to be?"

"I have the day off. I need to make some final calls to some of my military buddies, but I'll meet you at your apartment," Finn told her. He wasn't sure exactly what just happened, or what he'd agreed to. Was all the talk about sharing pieces of themselves a front for talking about if they were in a relationship or not? Addie didn't seem like the kind of girl that played games with that type of thing. She usually said what she meant, with no twisting of words or hidden meanings. That's one of the things he liked most about her.

"Okay. I'll see you then." She leaned up and pressed a kiss to his cheek.

He followed her out to the parking lot, watching the way she moved, then went for his truck. He could start on the phone calls now and be done in an hour. His first call was to his Sergeant-Major, Jack.

"Yeah?" Jack's gravelly voice came over the line.

Something akin to homesickness washed over Finn. Back in the Marines his life had been routine, he knew what he was doing every minute of the day and as the weeks went by. It was structured, orderly. But he couldn't stay there after Isaac died. "Sergeant-Major, it's Finn Thompson."

"How's civilian life treating you, Staff Sergeant?" Jack cleared his throat. "And none of the ranking nonsense, you're out of the life now."

"That's the thing, you know you're never really out of it." Finn talked small talk for a minute, listened to Jack talk about what was going on lately. Then he said, "Listen, has anything weird been going on out there? Maybe something that has to do with me or Isaac?"

"What's up, boy? You in some kind of trouble?" Jack's voice deepened in concern. He'd always treated the boys underneath him like they were his sons.

Finn took a deep breath. He still sat in the school parking lot and would need to start driving before someone reported him for being creepy. "I'm a fireman out in Sanctuary Bay on the east coast. Recently we've had some fires and two murders. Me and Isaac's tattoo was carved into the women's stomachs at the most recent fire and in the coffee table of a beach house fire a few weeks ago."

"That's some strange events," Jack stated.

What a fucking understatement. "The only people who really saw the tattoos were in the Marines. Maybe some girls we hung out with when we would go off base. I'm just trying to figure this mess out. See if someone has a grudge against me and is taking it out on innocent people."

"I'll get an unofficial investigation going over here, talk to the unit and find out who all has left the Marines and moved close to you or even people who've taken vacation out there. We'll find out who the bastard is."

Relief relaxed his shoulders. Sergeant-Major kept his word and worked doggedly until the task was finished to his standards. And his standards were high. "Thanks, sir."

"I'll get back to you."

As he hung up Finn pulled onto the main highway and headed toward Addie's. He called a few of his other contacts as he drove, but all had the same confusion the Sergeant-Major did. It was frustrating, but Finn hadn't really thought he'd find answers immediately. He'd just hoped for a miracle. When he reached Addie's, he knocked.

She opened the door and his gaze raked over her. With all the chaos churning around him, she was his lighthouse, his port in the storm to keep him grounded. He wasn't sure when he'd begun to feel that way, but it hit him with a force that almost knocked him off his feet.

"You okay?" Addie moved to the side to let him in.

"Mostly." Finn dipped his head down and kissed her, pulling her close after she shut the door. He didn't want to jump her as soon as he came over, he felt like he owed her more of an apology or something, but he couldn't resist a taste of her. After a minute, when he felt the desire simmering on the surface, he lifted his head and took a breath. It could get out of control in a hurry.

"Wow." Addie bit her lip.

Finn clenched his teeth, reminding himself that he wasn't going to push her onto her bed. That he wanted to spend some time with her, making sure everything was really okay between them. Women didn't just forgive that easily, there was always a catch.

"We can order some take out if you want." Addie bent down to pet Harlow, who wound around her ankles, purring.

"How about I cook?" Finn leaned against the kitchen counter. "I make a great chicken spaghetti."

Her eyes sparkled. "You want to cook me dinner? That's not too domestic for you?"

He knew the real question. It wasn't too relationship-like for him? His heart pounded in his chest, but he said, "No. Besides, you're going to die of a heart attack if you keep eating take-out every night."

"Hey, I eat at my parent's once in a while." She put her hands on her hips. Her mock rage was adorable and damn if he didn't want to kiss her nose.

"Doesn't count." He grinned. "I know the recipe by heart. Ready to go to the store?"

Addie glanced down at her athletic shorts and t-shirt, then shrugged. "Sure. Let's go."

They climbed into his truck and he drove toward the store.

"Since you've met my family, when will I get to meet yours?" Addie turned to look at him.

By the tone of her voice, he knew she was teasing but it still sent a shock running through him. He wasn't sure that was something he wanted. Meeting Kelsey would be okay, but Jenna? She was a trouble all her own. Maybe he could arrange something with Kelsey.

"Relax, Finn. I'm joking. If you don't want me to meet them, it's cool." Addie smiled at him. "Seriously. You look like I stunned you with a Taser."

Finn laughed softly. "It shocked me for a minute. It's just that one of my sisters is bat shit insane, and the other is really sweet. I'd prefer for you to meet one, but not the other."

"I can handle bat shit insane," Addie told him.

"Not this one." Finn sent her a quick glance. "You probably could, but I'm not ready for that yet."

Her laughter sounded through the cab of the truck and it echoed into his bones. He was sliding and not sure he could stop it. Even if he wanted to.

Chapter Twenty-Three

Addie

Something had changed in their pseudo-relationship. She couldn't quite say what it was, but she could feel the tenuous link between them. When he'd left this morning she'd been confused, and a little hurt, even though she figured it was about everything that was going on. Then he'd apologized to her, and she fell right back into him. It's not like she could help it. He was addicting.

She watched him walk in front of her for a second before running to catch up as he passed through the door to the store. It was fairly busy, since everyone was swinging by after work. People lined the aisles and more than one person had a disgruntled look on their face when they got blocked on an aisle.

Finn found a cart and started in the fresh produce section. She watched as he grabbed tomatoes, Chile peppers and bell peppers, then walked toward the meats.

He got a package of chicken breasts, and they moved on to a different aisle. Plenty of times they had to wait on people to move out of the way and Addie's patience wore thin. People were freaking everywhere and it seemed like it was their mission to get in everyone else's way.

"Finn! What are you doing here?"

Addie turned at the sound of the screeching voice and froze. What was the little whore that ruined Halle's life doing here? What the hell was she doing calling Finn's name? Addie looked back at him and saw his brows together and his lips turned down into a frown. She turned back to the blonde as she stopped in front of them. The girl barely spared a glance for Addie, instead threw her arms around Finn. Addie's brows rose as her temper did. Was he sleeping with her?

"Jenna, please let go." Finn pushed her arms down. "Don't act like you're happy to see me."

That peaked Addie's interest. Did she leave him? Was he only using Addie as a rebound? Addie's stomach churned and she hated that any of this mattered to her. This was why she didn't get involved with a man. Shit like this happened.

"Why would I be mad at you?" Jenna pouted. She tilted her head up at Finn.

Addie's fists balled at her sides and she slowly counted in her head. She couldn't attack this woman. It would mean Finn meant too much to her.

"We can talk about this later. As you can see, I'm with someone." Finn nodded his head at Addie.

"Oh, silly me. Hi." Jenna held out a hand. "I'm Finn's whore sister."

Addie's heart stopped. She didn't know what to say about that, but didn't reach her hand out. "I'm Addie, Halle's sister."

Jenna's smiled evaporated and she looked at the ground. "Oh. Um, I have to go."

Finn looked between them. "Your sister's ex is the one Jenna slept with?"

"That's one of the sisters that live here?" Addie countered.

Finn sighed, and pulled the cart off to a corner. Addie reluctantly followed him. She wasn't sure what this meant, although she couldn't deny that she was vastly relieved he hadn't been sleeping with her, but it raised a bigger question. If she and Finn ever got serious, how would she deal with the fact that Jenna was his sister?

"Look, I know that Jenna is tough to deal with--" He held a hand up when Addie tried to speak. "And that she broke up your sister's marriage. I don't want this to ruin anything that you and I have."

Addie shook her head. "This is a big deal. It might not seem like it, but damn it! She tore my sister apart. And while I know she wasn't the only one he slept with, she's the one that Halle saw fucking her husband in the office." Addie shut her eyes, trying to get the vision of Halle's devastated face out of her mind. Of how Halle was miserable still from what happened. What would Halle say when Addie told her?

"Let's get the rest of the supplies for dinner. You still want me to cook?" His eyes were solemn and she knew he was asking more than that.

She thought about not seeing him ever again. Her heart dropped, an emotion she never experienced before running through her. "Yes. I still want you to cook me dinner."

Relief and a little bit of hope shone in his eyes. "Okay, let's grab the rest of the stuff and get out of here. If you want to talk more about it, we can at your apartment."

Addie followed him around as he put the rest of the ingredients in the cart. Her eyes never left him as he moved, roaming over his face, his shoulders and arms, and his back as he reached for stuff. She wasn't sure, but she thought she was addicted to him. Would she be able to handle the withdrawal when the time came?

He paid for the stuff and she helped him carry it out to the truck. Neither one said a word on the way back to her apartment and the silence strained around them, ringing in her ears. Why did he have to be related to Jenna? Why did being with a guy have to be so damn complicated?

She offered to help carry the bags to her apartment but he shooed her to the stairs. Once inside Harlow meowed non-stop until Addie reached down and picked her up, nuzzling the sweet kitten. The kitten was growing fast and didn't fit in the palm of her hand anymore. She walked to Harlow's food bowl and refilled it and the water by the time Finn made it inside.

He stared at her for a minute but before she could ask why, he asked, "Where are all your cooking things?"

"What do you need? Mom stocked the place when I moved in, probably in hopes that I would use the stuff. You may know as much as I do where they are."

"You're so domestic, Addie." Finn winked at her, then searched through cabinets and drawers for what he needed. He started a pot of water to boil and put the chicken in there. "So, do we need to talk about this?"

Addie lifted a shoulder in a shrug. "What really is there to talk about? She's your sister, it's not like you can change the fact. Or what happened."

"I know, but I could tell you were shocked and a little angry by it." He started chopping the peppers and chilies while he talked.

"I was. Not at you, once I found out she was your sister."

He threw his head back and laughed.

Addie narrowed her eyes at him. "Hey, I had no idea she was your damn sister."

"My other sister, Kelsey, is much sweeter. I promise," he said when he finally finished laughing. "You don't have to hang out with Jenna, but I would like you to meet Kelsey."

"I don't know." Her mind had changed a bit once she saw Jenna. "You really want me to meet her?"

He looked at her over the bar, searing her with the intensity of the look. "Yes."

Addie sighed. "Fine, I will. But only Kelsey. I don't want to see Jenna right now. I'm not sure I could handle that." She had to text Victoria, Gemma, and Autumn to see what they thought about this situation.

"I can live with that." Finn nodded toward the fridge. "Why don't you get us some beers and we can talk about something else. I don't really want to talk about Jenna either. She's a pain in my ass. In everyone's ass, it seems."

After getting the beers, Addie slid onto a stool at the bar and once again caught herself watching him move. She didn't know if it was his time in the Marines or on the fire department, but he moved with confidence and grace she lacked. Confidence had never really been a big problem for her, but moving without running into something or dropping stuff--not her thing. She thanked God if she made it through a day without adding another bruise to her body. He was focused on his task, but any time she asked a question he answered it. It was weird to have a guy pay that much attention to her, one who really cared what she had to say. Her aversion to relationships slid down a notch.

Chapter Twenty-Four

Finn

He tried not to let on that her watching him made him hot. He knew it wasn't just the heat from cooking, it was the heat in her stares. She didn't hide the fact that she wanted him and it was refreshing. The fact that they saw his sister in the store had to give her some pause, he knew that she was upset about it. To him it didn't feel like a hurdle they couldn't get over, but he could understand her reticence.

Every time he glanced up from cooking she was watching him, eyes hooded and full of desire. For the first time he was reluctant to just throw her in bed. He wanted to get to know her. What she liked and didn't like. The type of music she listened to, what made her laugh and what made her cry. God, he didn't ever want to make her cry. Female tears undid him, especially if he was the one to cause them.

"Tell me more about your family." Addie propped her

chin on her fist and stared at him.

"You know I have four sisters. Kelsey and Jenna are the youngest. Sara and Laura are the oldest. I come in at the middle. My mom is a nurse and my dad is retired military. Marines, like me." Finn started. "We moved around a lot, finally settling in Chicago whenever he got out. Sara and Laura are both married, and I have one niece and nephew, both from Laura. Sara isn't sure she wants kids yet."

"That's a big family. I bet it was noisy during Christmas time."

"It was. Jenna and Kelsey moved here a year ago, and when I was honorably discharged I moved to be with them." He paused, wondering if he could get the rest out. "Kelsey and Isaac were engaged and when he didn't come home, I wasn't the only one devastated. Kelsey needed me, so I hired on with the SBFD as quick as I could."

"You're one sweet big brother." Addie's smile got brighter and warmed some of the coldness inside of him at the memory of Isaac's death. "I'm sure Kelsey appreciates you being here."

"She paints. Beautiful pictures. I think it's how she works through her grief."

Addie's look softened. "She sounds like someone I would like very much."

Something in Finn nearly broke when Addie said that. He knew how much she couldn't stand Jenna, but wanting to meet his other sister--his favorite sister--made him want to scoop her up and take her to the room. Show his appreciation for her in a lot of ways.

She noticed the look on his face and put a hand up. "Oh no. I'm hungry and that food smells delicious. You can wait until after I eat."

He laughed, feeling lighter than he had in a long time. How she did that to him, he didn't know. One touch, or kiss, or smile, and the darkness inside him receded just a little more each time. She was becoming a life line. He wasn't sure how dangerous that was at the moment, but decided he'd deal with it later. There was too much going on right now. He wasn't going to think about Isaac's death or the arson murders tonight. He wanted to focus on Addie.

They ate at the bar, side by side, talking about their day. He explained to her about his conversations with his Sergeant-Major and some of his old contacts from the military. She listened and asked a few questions of her own. Her insight was valuable and he made a note to present them to the Chief and his Sergeant-Major. After dinner, she helped with the dishes, laughing about how her mom would freak if she knew she was. They decided to watch some TV, cuddled on the couch, with Harlow on her lap.

He didn't really focus on what was on the screen, instead he focused on the feel of Addie. She had such a warm and caring personality, wrapped in a shell of who-the-hell-cares. He couldn't believe that he'd ever thought she was like Mia. They were worlds apart. While Mia never cared about anything but herself, he'd seen Addie put other people first constantly. It was admirable.

"Let's go to the room." Addie stood, pulling on his arm. "I can't wait any more. Sitting next to you, not doing anything, it's killing me."

He grinned. "You don't have to wait."

They barely made it past her doorway before she was unbuttoning his jeans. He tripped over the leg of his pants, but managed to keep himself upright. His hands traveled from her waist, up to her breasts and he groaned at the feel of them. They were swollen and warm, and he wanted a taste.

She pushed him onto the edge of the bed and yanked his jeans off. "Take off your boxers."

He did as she commanded, not caring that she was still clothed and he was naked. He took his shirt off, too, and tossed it aside. Before he knew it, she was on her knees in front of him, licking her lips. His cock jerked as her warm breath brushed over it and he saw her smile in amusement.

She wrapped a hand around the base and his breathing hitched. Her hands were soft but held him firmly. Her dark mass of hair was down, brushing his thighs, and his balls tightened. He wasn't sure he was going to survive this.

She glanced up at him, not looking away, as she leaned in and took him into her mouth. His fists tightened in the covers as he fought himself from digging them in her hair and taking control. He didn't think she'd like that. Her tongue swirled around the tip before she took him in again.

"Jesus Christ, Addie." Finn choked out.

Her other hand cradled his balls. She rolled them around in the palm of her hand, increasing the pressure on the base of his cock.

Liquid desire shot through him and he had to remind himself to breathe. That it was necessary for him to do that. She alternated using her hand and her mouth, the different sensations had him bucking. Her hands left his cock and balls and pushed on his thighs to keep in him place, which made him want to explode.

Before he couldn't take it anymore, he wrapped his hands in her hair, pulling her off of him.

"I need you. Right now." Finn shoved her shorts and

panties down, didn't even worry about her shirt and bra. She straddled him, immediately sinking down. He clenched his teeth to keep from coming right there. She had to explode, too. His teeth and lips nibbled at her neck as he made sure and slow strokes inside of her.

Her walls clenched around him and he cursed into her neck. She laughed softly, leaning back to create a deeper angle.

His control snapped. Moving quick and hard, he drove his hips into hers. She gripped his shoulders, her eyes wide. Each thrust seemed to pull more and more of his soul out of the darkness. The light was almost blinding as she came around him, whispering his name softly, like she couldn't live without him.

He finally let go, thrusting against her until he couldn't move. His breath rasped inside his chest and his heart raced. He felt so alive, so peaceful that he didn't want to move yet.

Addie touched her forehead to his, breathing just as heavily. There was something different in her gaze, but he wasn't sure if he was just seeing what he wanted to. If he was putting emotions in her expressions that weren't there. Damn, he needed to figure out what he wanted from her. He was sliding deeper and didn't know if she felt the same way.

Chapter Twenty-Five

Addie

She needed to talk to her sisters about everything that was going on with Finn, and tell Halle about Jenna, but she wanted to talk to Victoria first. So she met Victoria at her office after school was out, the girls having been picked up by their grandmother. Victoria's sleek and elegant office suited her perfectly. It was also across from the boardwalk and the beach, so it was in a prime location.

Ella greeted her as Addie walked in, waving from behind her desk. She was Victoria's assistant and loved her job, had a sweet demeanor, and helped Victoria out a lot. Her brown hair was pulled into an elegant bun and she wore a yellow dress and pumps that suited her.

"Hey, Addie." Ella came around the desk. "She's with a client but the meeting should be over in a few minutes. How're you doing?"

"Good, school's back in, so it's chaotic during the day.

My wine consumption has doubled." Addie laughed.

"I'd drink a lot, too, if I dealt with kids all day." Ella took a seat behind the desk. "I'm an only child, so kids freak me out."

"They can freak me out sometimes, too. Kids have special ways of doing that. I don't know how many times I've had to have parent conferences for the weirdest stuff."

Ella wrinkled her nose. "I can only imagine."

Victoria walked out of her office, dressed in a slim white dress and heels, something she only wore when she had client appointments. She escorted the lady out the door, assuring her that she'd begin work on the lady's home soon. When the lady was gone, Victoria turned to Addie. "What's going on?"

Addie blew out a breath. "I need to talk to you."

"It's time for my break anyway. I'll go hit some of the shops on the boardwalk." Ella smiled at the sisters. "Just text me when you're done, Victoria, and I'll head back."

"Come on." Victoria led the way to her office.

Addie settled into a chair, Victoria taking the one across from her, instead of sitting behind the desk. She wondered if she should tell her about the Lucia stuff, too. "Okay, so things with Finn have slowly been getting more serious."

Victoria's eyes widened. She remained silent, but

watched her sister closely.

"He stayed the night last night and cooked me dinner. We got ready for work this morning--*together*--and left at the same time. We ate breakfast and drank coffee. Again--*together*." Addie suddenly felt like something extremely heavy was sitting on her chest. She stood and paced the room.

"Sweetie, it sounds like you really like him." Victoria followed her movements.

"I might. But there's something else. His freaking sister is the whore who slept with Trevor. The one that Halle walked in on." Addie threw her hands up in the air. "What the fuck am I supposed to do with that? What will Halle say? It's bound to hurt her and I don't want to reopen those wounds."

"Sit down, you're giving me anxiety." Victoria waited on her to sit before she continued, "First of all, Halle is a big girl. She's going to recognize how you feel about Finn. At first it may be awkward, but she won't let that get in the way of you being happy. Second, Trevor is the one that hurt her, not Finn. She isn't going to hold it against him."

Addie balked when Victoria mentioned feelings for Finn. She didn't have emotional feelings for him, right? It was all physical. Shit, who was she kidding? "What do I do with this?" Her eyes beseeched Victoria to give her some advice.

"With the girl or with your feelings for Finn?" Victoria smiled softly at Addie's panicked expression. "We'll talk to Halle about the girl. What do you want to do about your feelings? I can give you advice, but ultimately what you do with them is up to you. I know it scares the hell out of you, but it's the first time you've ever felt this way. I think it's good for you."

"How is this good for me?" Addie shot Victoria a dark look. "I'm terrified of what I'm feeling. I feel like I'm on uneven ground that could open up at any minute and swallow me whole. Not to mention the fact that I wait on him to call, or text, or show up. I've *never* done that before."

"That's why it's good for you. He's opened up those walls and is causing you to actually *feel* something, and that's what scares you. You're going to have to take a leap of faith. I remember how hard it was for me when I met Nick, especially after what Roger did. It was so hard to open back up, but for the right person, it's worth it."

"Ugh, I'm going to die. I don't think I can handle this." Addie groaned and started to pace again. "Life was so simple before him. I liked how it was. I was independent and had all this free time to myself."

"But now that you've met him, would you take it back? Go on without meeting him?"

Addie paused. The thought of him not being in her life made her chest hurt. Misery coiled around it. "Shit."

Victoria laughed at the wonder on her sister's face. "You've got it bad, girl."

Addie thought about that on the way home. Halle was coming over in a little while, and so was Victoria. Tonight she was telling each of her sisters something they probably didn't want to hear. She raced up the stairs to her apartment and sent Finn a text letting him know that she had something with her sisters tonight. He replied, saying that he had to work at the station.

Her apartment felt strangely empty without him as she moved to get the wine and glasses out. These conversations would definitely need some liquid courage to go with it. She changed out of her work clothes, then cleaned out Harlow's litter box. Anything to keep herself busy until they arrived.

They both walked in at the same time, laughing and cheery. God, Addie hoped they would leave that way. Not mad at her or at the world. She poured the wine, making sure they each had enough to get through this. Her stomach was queasy and she hoped she could keep the wine down.

Halle and Victoria sat at the bar.

"What is going on with you?" Halle gave Addie a thorough look over. "You look sick. Are you pregnant?"

"Holy shit, no. Halle, don't you curse me." Some of the tension melted away as she laughed. "No. I'm not. But since you asked that, I guess I'll talk with Victoria first."

"Oh God." The color drained from Victoria's face. "What the hell is going on?"

Addie glanced at Halle, then back at Victoria. "Lucia talked with me a while back about something, and she swore me to secrecy. I discussed it with Halle, because I wasn't sure if the topic was serious enough to breach that trust with Lucia."

Victoria fanned herself, trying to get more color back in her cheeks. "What kind of conversation?" She took a long sip of her wine.

"Um." Addie took a deep breath. "Well, some of the other girls on the cheer squad have already lost their V-card and are pressuring Lucia to do it."

"What?" Victoria jumped off the stool. "You two didn't think that was important enough to tell me then? Jesus, Addie. That's a big deal!"

"I know." Addie held up her hands to placate her sister.

"We should've told you. I talked with her and I think I impressed on her the importance of waiting. That it's a special moment that should be with a special guy. Not a guy that she barely likes."

Victoria's face was splotched with red and she took several deep breaths. "This is unbelievable. She's only thirteen. Why is she worried about that already?" A thought occurred to her, and she looked back at Addie. "Has Helena said anything about this?"

"No, Helena is only worried about school right now."

"Thank God." Victoria muttered. "I can't believe you kept this from me for so long. What if she'd slept with him? What if she did? Oh God." Victoria drained the rest of her wine.

"If I thought she was going to do that, to take that step, I promise I would've told you immediately. I just didn't want to break her trust, because she'll never tell me anything again." Addie soothed.

"Why couldn't she tell me? I'm not a bad mother." Victoria frowned and Addie saw the hurt in her eyes. She quickly rounded the corner and put her arms around Victoria.

"She didn't tell you because she respects you too much and doesn't want to disappoint you. She was probably afraid of your reaction. I don't think she held back because you're a bad mother, because you're not. You're the best mother besides ours."

"That's the truth," Halle put in. "You've done so much for those girls, and you love them to pieces. She wasn't trying to hurt you."

"Okay. Just next time, please tell me immediately. I promise not to track her down and go off on her. But I also need to communicate with her, show her that there's nothing she could do that would disappoint me. She should feel able to tell me anything, that's what I'm for." Victoria looked to Halle. "Now, we have something to tell you."

Halle's face closed down. "What?"

"Just say it, Addie. It's easier that way," Victoria said.

Addie's stomach was a tortuous mess of misery. How would Halle react to this? "Finn is Jenna's brother." She knew she didn't have to explain further when Halle's face paled. "I know what it looks like, and I swear that I didn't know when I met him. I can stop seeing him if you want."

"Shut up, Addie." Halle didn't say it unkindly. "I just need a minute to adjust."

Addie stared at her hands, not able to see the rejection in Halle's eyes. She was facing the prospect of never seeing Finn again and her heart fought the idea. When had she come to care so much about him?

"It's not Finn's fault that his sister is a whore." Halle took a deep breath. "I've met him remember? At Luke's football party? He was kind and sweet and very polite. Not once did I get a bad vibe from him. And the fact that you even brought this to me without just breaking up with him first tells me how much you already feel for him. I'm not going to stand in the way of that."

"Thank you." Addie hugged Halle close, loving her sister for her selflessness. "I won't ever invite her to any family events, I promise."

"Good, because I'd have to kill you." Halle brushed a tear from her cheek and smiled at them. "Now, let's talk about something happy. I think we all need it."

Chapter Twenty-Six

Finn

A few days later, Jack called him back. Three guys from his former unit were vacationing on the eastern seaboard and it just so happened that all three had a problem with him while he was there for one reason or another.

The first was Steven Marshall, a guy that Finn busted with drugs while on base. Steven lost two ranks and served 30 days. Ever since then, Steven disliked Finn. Sergeant-Major told him that Steven had taken a leave of absence two months ago. The second was Todd Aldrich, whose offense was a little more personal. While Finn was dating Mia, Todd developed a hard-on for her and got a chance to bang her. When Mia didn't leave Finn for Todd, Todd reacted harshly. He'd caused trouble for Finn overseas, petty pranks and arguments. He'd never attacked Finn outright, so Finn had trouble seeing him as an arsonist.

The third was Roy Smith. This one was a little more serious. Finn had caught him stealing stuff from the villagers. One night he and Isaac had stopped Roy from raping a twelve year old girl. When questioned about it, they stood up for the girl and Roy was dishonorably discharged.

Finn ended the call with his Sergeant-Major and looked around the fire station. His friends were in a game of pool, and he could hear Carter teasing Caleb about the time Autumn had beat the fire out of him. If Roy was the one causing this, and Finn could clearly see him doing it, were his friends in danger by being near him? Roy was violent and had no regard for rules or morals. He'd asked the Sergeant-Major to look further into each one and see where exactly they were and why they were each on vacation. He just couldn't believe he didn't think about these men sooner.

Next, he needed to talk to the Chief. He'd wanted to stay apprised of the situation, but since he wasn't in at the moment, Finn would have to wait to tell him. He thought back to all the times he'd confronted those guys, each memory a little distant, and pretended to watch his friends play pool. It just didn't make any sense. Why was the arsonist attacking him now, after so long? Each of those incidents happened over a year ago.

Why fire? He couldn't think of anything that tied those men to fire. None had ever exhibited any symptoms of being a pyromaniac, although they could have hidden it.

"Finn, want to play?" Carter broke him from his thoughts.

Finn shook his head. His energy wasn't really in playing games right now. Not when two women were dead. Even if it wasn't necessarily his fault, it was directed at him.

"Do you like my necklace?" Aaron stood from the couch and held it up. "My sister gave it to me."

Not wanting to be a dick, Finn took a deep breath and looked at the silver necklace. From the thin chain hung a black dragon with wings arched out as if it was going to take flight. "Cool. You're sister picked a good one."

"Yeah, she did." Aaron grinned. "She said I remind her of a dragon."

Finn didn't know what to say to that, just nodded, and then walked to the fridge.

Carter handed the pool stick to Nate and walked over to Finn. "Is everything okay?"

Finn thought about telling Carter and realized he wanted to. Carter was a true friend, and Finn felt that at least he deserved to know. If it came down to it, he'd tell the whole unit. "Let's talk over here." He led Carter to the garage bay.

Carter watched him carefully, his face serious. "Did something happen?"

"Those women from the last fire? They had my tattoo carved into their stomachs." Finn jumped right into it, didn't feel like sugarcoating it.

Carter frowned but stayed silent.

"It got me thinking, so I checked photos from the beach house fire a few weeks ago. My tattoo was carved into the coffee table." Finn leaned against the concrete wall, wanting some type of balance as he talked. Everything felt unstable around him. "This tattoo was from my time in the Marines. I got it with my best friend, Isaac." He swallowed the lump in his throat. "He died in Afghanistan."

"I'm sorry, Finn." Carter glanced down at the tattoo. "So you're saying that someone from your time in the military is doing this?"

"That's the only thing I can think of. No one else really knew about the tattoo, not it's meaning or the significance of it. People here barely notice it."

"Have you talked to anyone from that time?"

"Yeah. I got the names of three guys that are on vacation out here somewhere from my old Sergeant-Major.

Three guys that all have a reason to hate me." Finn relayed to Carter what Jack told him.

After a moment of silence, Carter looked Finn in the eyes. "What do we need to do?"

"I'm not getting you mixed up in this. Two women have already been killed because of me."

"Because of the son of a bitch that killed them. Not because of you." Carter stepped forward. "You have to understand that. You are not the guilty one here. We're going to find out who's behind this."

"Damn it, I'm serious. I don't want anyone else getting hurt."

"It's too late. You're my friend, you don't get to do this alone," Carter said. "Now, when the Chief gets here we can both talk to him. We'll figure this out together."

Finn watched him walk away, marveling at the fact that he wasn't alone. He may have felt that way, but all around him were people that cared about him, about what happened to him.

The Chief arrived the next morning. All was silent from the arsonist's front, which worried Finn even more. He and Carter met the Chief in the office, where Finn explained what he'd learned about viable suspects.

"Does your Sergeant-Major know where exactly these

men are?" Chief leaned back in his chair. He looked longingly at his empty coffee cup.

Finn ignored it for a moment. The Chief could wait a few minutes for his morning caffeine. "Not yet. He's looking into it. He has a friend at the FBI who is checking the men's backgrounds. Only one is still in the Marines, although he's doing a piss poor job there."

"You brought Carter into this?" Chief eyed Finn.

"No, sir. I brought myself into it. Finn tried to keep me away, but I hassled him until he told me."

"Alright. So what do you think we should do from here?" Chief asked.

"First, I need to know who is even in this area. If the Sergeant-Major doesn't call me back this afternoon, I'll call him."

"I'd like to see the photos from the beach house." Carter placed his elbows on his knees and leaned forward. "I want to get a feel for what the guy's thinking."

Chief took the folder out of the drawer and handed them over.

Carter frowned when he got to the photo of Finn's tattoo carved into the coffee table. "We really need those background files. It could give us a good lead as to who the arsonist is. Usually they aren't that great at hiding the symptoms. A little fire here, a vandalism with fire there."

"We just have to wait and see what the Sergeant-Major digs up." Finn let his impatience thread into his voice. He didn't want anymore innocent people to die because of him.

Chapter Twenty-Seven

Addie

Okay, it was time to admit she missed him. Addie couldn't deny it any longer. She well and truly missed Finn. His voice, his laugh, the little crooked smile when she did something he thought was cute. His touch…Jesus, she sounded like a freaking high school girl. It wasn't like she could help it. She waited this long to become attached to someone, so her mind and body were catching up.

He was coming over after his shift ended at the station, which was around seven. It was only six o'clock now. She heaved a sigh and decided that maybe her room could use some cleaning up. As she surveyed the room, hands on hips, she realized she should've been embarrassed the times he stayed the night. She was a messy person. No denying that either.

Harlow trailed after her, pawing at her feet, as she gathered the myriad piles of dirty clothes and actually put them in the clothes hamper. She laughed a little, knowing that if her mother saw her doing this, she'd probably faint. Once that was finished, she picked up all the empty soda cans that littered her nightstand and threw them away. After they were cleared off, she saw the sticky residue they left and wiped the nightstand down. It was a miracle she didn't have ants.

She put fresh sheets on her bed, then folded her clean clothes and put them away.

"I didn't realize I had this much room in here. Or a floor." Addie kneeled down to pet Harlow a few times. The kitten meowed at her, nuzzling her hand. "Finn better get here soon or I may clean the whole apartment. Imagine that."

She started a load of clothes in the washer and then made herself stop. If liking a guy and waiting on him made her this fidgety, how was she going to make it if they made things serious? Did she want to make things serious? Already she realized that not seeing him ever again made her sick, so what exactly did that mean? How did a person know if love was really love or just a hyperactive case of lust?

Most of the relationships she saw crumbled into ashes, with the exception of her parents. She'd watched them growing up, and while their marriage wasn't perfect, they were still in love. It was evident in the way they talked, kissed, or looked at each another.

How does someone walk through that fire? Just get through the other side without burning to those ashes? What made a relationship stick?

It's not like she'd know. Finn was the first guy she'd ever dated for longer than a weekend. When that sentence didn't cause her heart to race in panic, she knew she was done for. So much of her life was changing and it was all because of him.

He knocked on the door and she sighed in relief. He could distract her from her thoughts, even if they were about him. When she opened the door, he kissed her softly. She leaned in, breathing his scent. It comforted her.

"You cooking tonight?" He laughed when she shot him a look. "I figured. Want Chinese?"

"Sounds good to me." Addie shut the door behind him. He looked right at home here and she freaked just a tiny bit at that.

"How was your day?" Finn dug through her menu drawer and pulled the Chinese one out.

Her lips quirked at that. It was such a normal, relationship question. "Good. We're having end of the quarter testing soon, since it's already the beginning of October. The kids had to start doing their study guides. They're not happy about it."

"Who would be? Know what you want?" He waved the menu.

"I want sweet and sour chicken with fried rice and wontons on the side." She glanced over the menu. "It's a number 12."

"Okay. I'll call it in."

She sat on the couch, watching him as he did. He moved surely, and she knew that confidence translated to how he moved in bed. Faint lines of stress creased his brow and she wondered just how much all this was getting to him. He was the kind of guy who would blame this all on himself, even when it wasn't his fault. It was like she could almost see the weight of the events heavy on his shoulders.

He finished the call and looked up, gaze meeting hers. A ghost of a smile crossed his lips. "What is it?"

"You're letting this hang about you. Thinking too hard about it. I can almost see your mind turning in circles, and I think you're hampering your ability to figure this out."

"It's not like I can just shut it off." He sank down beside her. Instantly the heat from his body warmed her where they touched.

"I know." She placed her hand on the side of his face, rubbed the stubble there. "I don't want you to wear yourself into the ground either."

This time she got a full smile. "You sound like you care what happens to me."

Her heartbeat faltered. She couldn't say what she didn't fully realize yet, but she let the emotion show in her eyes. And what she showed, she saw mirrored in his. His head leaned down and he kissed her, but kept it from boiling over since the food would be there soon.

After a few minutes of sinking into the kiss, he leaned back and said, "Sergeant-Major got in touch with me. We have three suspects now. All are men from my past in the military and all three are vacationing out here somewhere."

"Does he know where?"

"Not yet, but he's looking into it." He rubbed a hand through his hair and she could see the tension in his body. "I want you to be extra careful. These men are dangerous and I don't want anything to happen to you."

The concern in his eyes almost undid her. It's what stopped her from scoffing at his sentence. "I will," she said softly.

"Good."

"What about your sisters?" Addie didn't really care

about Jenna, not that she wanted her to die in a fire, and even though she hadn't met Kelsey, she'd picked up on Finn's obvious affection for her.

"I've talked to them. God knows if Jenna will listen, but Kelsey will. They're just out there on the edge of town by themselves." He looked down at his hands, where they were balled into fists.

"You should stay with them tonight. It would make you feel better," she suggested, even though the thought of him not staying disappointed her.

"What about you?"

"I can handle myself." Addie flexed an arm. "They'd be sorry they even tried."

His lips quirked and he tested her muscle. "Yeah, I bet they would. I'll eat with you and then head out to their house. Are you sure you don't mind?"

Addie kept the disappointment out of her tone when she replied, "I'm sure."

She listened to him tell her about how Carter now knew what was going on, and how the Sergeant-Major had an FBI buddy helping out. She hoped this would be over soon. Whoever the arsonist was, he'd already murdered two women. What would happen if he decided his game with Finn was over?

Chapter Twenty-Eight

Finn

A week passed with nothing to show for the arsonist. The FBI agent that Jack knew had gotten back to him. Steven Marshall was in Tampa, FL so that ruled him out. He wouldn't have time to get back and forth from where he was. Roy Smith had yet to be found, but the agent was still looking. What really boiled his blood was that Todd Aldrich was vacationing in Virginia Beach.

A flash of anger hit Finn when he thought about the weekend he and Addie and their friends had gone down there. Was that fucker hanging around even then? Had he watched everything that had happened? If that man had laid eyes on Addie, with an intent to hurt her, he'd kill him.

Halloween was coming up in the next few weeks, and the town was busy in preparation. Unlike where he was from, Sanctuary Bay liked to throw itself fully into the tradition. Pumpkins and fall wreaths decorated porches and doors and window decorations were everywhere. Twice he'd gone to the store, hoping to pick up Reese's Peanut Butter cups, and the shelves were bare each time.

He had a shift for the next two days at the station and was disappointed that he wouldn't get to see Addie. With everything going on and him staying with his sisters when he wasn't at the station, time to spend with her had been sparse. He only hoped that when this was finally over, he could spend a lot more time with her.

"Finn, I need you to check the inventory tonight." Chief called from his office.

"Sure thing, Chief." Finn stood in his doorway.

"Get Carter and Caleb to help."

"Yes, sir."

He located them in the kitchen, snacking on some leftovers. "Chief wants us to work on inventory tonight."

"Damn." Caleb brushed his cheese coated fingers on his pants. "I hate inventory. It makes my eyes cross."

"Everything makes your eyes cross." Carter punched him in the shoulder. "It'll go faster with all three of us."

"Start in a few minutes?" Finn asked.

"Sure." They both agreed. Carter shot him an unreadable look and Finn just shook his head. Although he couldn't read the expression, he knew it had something to do with the arson case. Finn didn't want to pull anyone else into this. The more people that were involved, the more people who could get hurt.

He sent Addie a quick text, telling himself it was just to check on her and that he didn't really miss her *that* much. Then he started in the supply room, a clipboard in one hand and a pen in the other. Inventory was important because all of their supplies needed to be up to code. Going into a fire with defective equipment could be dangerous to all parties involved.

Carter and Caleb joined him soon after. They moved through the shelves, systematically checking the air masks, gloves, and boots for need of repair. It took a few hours and when Finn checked the time, it was past ten-thirty. He stopped, and when Carter and Caleb noticed, they stopped also.

While they took a fifteen minute break, Finn texted Addie and told her goodnight. She responded with a goodnight and that he better call her in the morning before she went to work. He couldn't help but smile at the commanding tone of the text. Somehow he'd gone from being wary of her fiery personality to admiring it.

When they went back to work, it was to check the hoses. Using sharp eyes and trailing fingers, they looked for wear and tear or holes. They checked the back up ones first, and then the ones on the trucks. The moon shone outside, and Finn's thoughts turned to Addie.

He shifted when his phone rang, putting the clipboard and pen down. The screen flashed Jenna's name and he answered.

"God, finally. Finn, something's wrong." Jenna's voice shook over the phone.

Finn's heart dropped. "What is it?" He didn't mean to snap, but worry made him anxious.

"The house…Jesus…it's a mess. I can't find Kelsey." Jenna's voice cracked. "The door was kicked in."

"You went into the house?" Finn took a deep breath when she sobbed. "I'm sorry, Jenna. I'm just worried about both of you. Did you call the cops?"

"Yes. Right before I called you. Finn, I need you." Jenna had never admitted it before, never asked for him.

"I'm on my way."

Carter and Caleb had heard his side of the conversation. "We're coming with you. I'll call the Chief on the way. Nate and Noah can come in."

"Someone has to stay here until they come." Finn walked out the door, his heart racing with apprehension. Where was Kelsey and who had her?

"I'll stay until they get here," Caleb said, "and I'll call the Chief. Go."

Finn and Carter got into Finn's truck and he sped out of the parking lot and down the road toward his sisters'. What the fuck was going on? Who wanted to hurt him through his sisters?

Blue and red lights flashed in the night as they approached. Finn slammed on the breaks by the curb. He noticed Carter let go of his death grip on the safety bar.

A cop standing at the door stopped them as they ran up. "I'm sorry, but you can't go in. It's a crime scene."

"Where is my sister?" Finn growled at the young guy.

"Finn?"

He spun around, saw Jenna standing by one of the police cars, another officer beside her. Finn ran over to her. Her face was streaked with tears and even before he hugged her, he could see her shaking. Damn it, he'd kill whoever scared her and took Kelsey. He just had to find them. "Are you okay?"

Jenna nodded against his chest. "Where's Kelsey?"

"I don't know. But I'm going to find out."

"Excuse me, sir. Who are you?" The police officer interrupted them.

"I'm her brother." Finn looked at him over Jenna's

head. His name tag read Dunnam.

Dunnam nodded. "Can we get a statement from you?"

"Sure. But I need to know if this is tied to my case? The one with the arsonist?" Finn clenched his jaw. He was wasting time out here when he should be inside figuring out what the hell was going on.

"Let me check with dispatch. Your name?"

"Finn Thompson. It's about an arsonist case. Someone's been stalking me, carving my tattoo into almost dead women and setting shit on fire. My chief and I spoke with Detective Krakowski last month about it."

"Okay, give me a minute." The office spoke with dispatch and then walked back over. "The detectives in charge of your case will be here in a few minutes."

"Kelsey may not have a few minutes!" Finn shouted. Jenna jumped in his arms and he rubbed her back to soothe her.

"Sir, I can't allow you in there," Dunnam called as Finn rushed past the officer at the door. Carter stood between the officers and the house, face menacing.

The broken door was lying to the side in the foyer. His stomach clenched when he saw the living room. The coffee table was on its side, a glass of wine soaked red into the rug. Pieces of its glass was scattered across the floor. Finn tried to block the image of someone hurting his sister from his mind.

Something caught his eye, and he knelt down to pick it up. It was a necklace, one that he knew didn't belong to his sisters. He picked it up, letting it twirl on the silver chain. Spotted the black dragon. "Son of a bitch."

Aaron had his sister.

He rushed back out of the house, stopping by Carter and holding up the necklace to the police.

"Holy shit. Is that Aaron's?" Carter's mouth set in a grim line.

"Yeah." Finn tossed it to Dunnam. "We need to figure out where he is."

Dunnam must've heard the threat in his tone, because he spoke into his radio.

Finn needed to find his sister and he needed to find her now.

Chapter Twenty-Nine

Addie

She got the call around 11:00pm and shot out of bed. Kelsey was missing, her house a wreck. She ignored the fact that Finn hadn't called her, that it came from Gemma, who'd heard through Carter. It was just because he was worried about Kelsey, and she would deal with that, but later. Now, she threw her hair up and pulled on some yoga pants.

Late at night the streets of Sanctuary Bay were empty. She went a little faster than she should have, following the address Gemma gave her, but she wanted to make sure Finn was okay. Soon, blue and red lights illuminated a house near the outskirts of town.

Once she stepped out of the car, the October chill hung in the air, and she wished she'd brought a light jacket. Gemma stood in a group with Carter and Caleb. Addie's mouth went dry when she saw Finn standing next to Jenna, an arm around her. From the way he stood, she could see the tension thrumming through him, the need to move--to do something.

Swallowing her distaste about Jenna, she stopped next to the group. The despair and anger in Finn's eyes shocked her. Not the despair as much, but that anger was fueled by something else. Was he angry that she was here? He stepped aside from Jenna for a second.

"Why are you here?" Even his voice sounded angry.

Addie blinked, ignoring his tone. He was worried and this was how he dealt with it. "Gemma called me. I came to help you."

He stared at her another few moments before his arms went around her. "Thank you for coming," he whispered into her hair.

"Of course." She stepped back, giving him room to move back to his sister.

He did, his arm going around her again. Jenna cast a look at Addie, but Addie looked away, not wanting to tempt fate by getting angry at one sister while the other was missing.

Gemma, Carter, and Caleb stood to the left and a group of police officers to the right. A detective in a suit scribbled furiously on a pad, shooting questions at Finn and Jenna every time he paused. Addie moved to Gemma, Carter, and Caleb.

"I called Autumn. She should be here in a few minutes." Gemma leaned into Carter and his arm went around her. "I know we probably can't do anything but we can be here for moral support."

"I can't believe Aaron would do this." Carter frowned, eyes sad. "He always seemed like a nice guy. He joked around with us, had fun. He never seemed to dislike Finn in any way."

"It's one of the guys you work with?" Addie glanced at Finn. He was looking at the house, a dark expression on his face. She shivered and had no doubt that if he beat the police to Aaron, the arsonist was dead.

"Yeah. Finn's Sergeant-Major and FBI friend are trying to locate Aaron now. They're tracing his phone. I'm not sure that will give him anything," Carter said.

"Was his tattoo anywhere?" Addie asked. She prayed that Aaron wasn't carving it into Kelsey. The thought made her stomach queasy.

"Finn said it was painted on the living room wall. When this is over, I'm going to help Gemma paint over it. Don't want the sisters having that reminder when they get back."

"That's sweet of you, Carter." Gemma's eyes softened

when she looked at him.

A crowd of people began to form. The officers started to move them back to the opposite side of the street. Addie wished they'd disappear, go back home. What did they expect to see?

Finn's phone rang and he dug it out of his pocket. His movements were sharp and quick, and he brought the phone to his ear. "Yeah?" He barked the question out. His eyes narrowed as he listened. Then he moved toward his truck, running, his face grim. The officers called out after him but he was already peeling out of the driveway and gone.

Addie's stomach rolled. He must've gotten Aaron's location and was going after him. But what about the police? Why didn't he let them handle it? She knew why, but damn it, she didn't want him in harm's way.

Two of the officers and the detective hopped in a patrol car and sped after him. Addie hoped they'd catch up and keep him safe. She shared an anxious look with Gemma.

Jenna stood there, shaking in the wind, her face forlorn. Addie wondered where Trevor was and why he wasn't here comforting her. Then she let go of that derisive thought and sighed. The girl was all alone, and even though she hated the thought of being nice to the girl who broke her sister's heart, Jenna was also Finn's sister. So she walked over to her, hating the manners her mother taught her. "Hey, would you like to come back with me to my apartment?"

Jenna looked at her, brows drawn in. "What?"

Addie sighed. "It doesn't mean we're going to be besties or that I even like you, but you're Finn's sister and I don't want to leave you here alone."

"I'll come with you, too," Gemma said. "Moral support. You don't mind, right?" She asked Carter.

"No, go ahead." Carter kissed her. "I'm going to wait here for Finn."

"Okay." Gemma turned to look at Addie and Jenna.

"Well?" Addie watched Jenna, waiting on her answer.

"Okay." Jenna deflated, like she thought that once she was at Addie's, she was going to be beat to death or something.

Addie felt a tiny smidge of pity and maybe that would keep her from lashing out at her. Jenna had enough to deal with at the moment. Before they walked to Addie's car, she spoke with an officer, letting him know that she was going to take Jenna to her apartment. The officer nodded and took her information, in case they needed to contact her.

She prayed it wouldn't be about Finn getting hurt. Or killing someone.

She and Gemma led Jenna to her car. Unfortunately she'd parked where the loads of people gathered. An officer stood on the other side of her car, keeping people from bumping up against it. After unlocking the doors, she let Gemma and Jenna get in before walking around to the driver's side.

A woman grabbed her arm. Addie jerked her head up. "Excuse me?"

"I'm sorry. I just wanted to make sure everyone was all right." The woman had light brown hair and hazel eyes, which were full of concern.

Addie pulled her arm away, worry for Finn and Kelsey making her short with the woman and moved to get in the car. "It's really none of your business."

The woman narrowed her eyes at Addie's brusque tone.

Chapter Thirty

Finn

His hands gripped the steering wheel so hard his fingers ached. Questions swirled like a tornado in his mind as he thought about why Aaron would want to hurt him or his sister. He flew down the road, going at least 80, knowing that the cops weren't far behind.

Jack had called and told him where Aaron was. It didn't surprise him to find out that Aaron had taken Kelsey to the fire station, but now he worried about his crew along with his sister. It seemed fitting, even if Finn didn't understand what the hell was going on. It blew him away that Aaron was the arsonist. He'd been so sure that it was someone from his past, someone from the military who knew about his tattoo.

Either way the guy was fucked up. Mentally and soon to be physically. He wouldn't get away with scaring his sisters and if he so much as made Kelsey shed a damn tear, he was going to rip him to pieces.

The fire station was close and Finn jerked the steering wheel, flying into the parking lot. His heart thudded in his chest. The fire station was dark as he got out of his truck and he could hear sirens in the distance and knew the police would be here soon. Moving quietly, he headed into the garage bay. Where would Aaron take his sister?

He almost tripped, his foot connecting with something. Using his phone as a flashlight, he illuminated the floor. Breath rushed from his lungs. Nate and Noah lay on the ground, bleeding from both their heads. He leaned over them, checking both their pulses and heaved a sigh of relief. Both men were alive, but he wasn't sure how much longer Kelsey would be.

He moved around them, shutting the light off on his phone. Giving away his position would only help Aaron. Finn knew the firehouse like the back of his hand, he could navigate it in the dark. His training in the Marines immediately came back to him, not like he'd forgotten, and he crouched low, moving toward the living room and kitchen area.

The problem was, Aaron was just as familiar with the firehouse.

He heard a muffled scream and froze. It was coming

from the bunk room upstairs. A cold sweat broke out on his skin. That was Kelsey screaming, which meant that bastard was hurting her. Without thinking, he ran to the stairs, skirting the pool table, and took them two at a time.

The light came on upstairs, beckoning him closer. He burst into the bunkroom and slid to a stop.

Aaron had Kelsey tied to the bed in only her bra and panties. Blood ran down her sides from where Aaron had started on his tattoo. Her eyes, wide with fear and pain, set off the paleness of her skin, and from where he stood Finn could see her body vibrating. His fists clenched at his sides, and his jaw clenched so hard he thought he might chip his teeth.

"I thought you'd never get here." Aaron's lips twisted into a macabre grin.

"What the fuck is your problem?" Finn forced himself to stay where he was. A knife dangled from Aaron's fingertips and at the manic look in his eyes, he wouldn't hesitate to use it if Finn moved.

"What do you mean?" Aaron twirled the knife over Kelsey's body and she whimpered.

Finn met her terrified gaze and tried to show his determination to get her safe. He was getting her out of this no matter the cost to himself. Seeing her, seeing the blood, brought back sharp memories of the war that he fought to keep in check. Now was not the time to lose his head to flashbacks. He had to get her out of here.

"Why are you attacking me? Why my sister?"

"Oh," Aaron glanced down at Kelsey. "She's very pretty and you annoy the hell out of me." He returned his attention to Finn, eyes hard and blazing with jealousy.

That shocked Finn. Why would anyone be jealous of him? He was a broken mess and he never bothered anyone. "Why? I've never done anything to you."

The sirens sounded closer now and stopped whenever the police pulled into the parking lot. It didn't seem to faze Aaron, he kept his eyes on Finn.

"You have always been in the way. Always." Aaron gestured with the knife. Kelsey flinched.

Finn breathed in through his nose and out through his mouth, trying to stay calm. He had to keep Aaron's focus on him.

"All she can see is you," Aaron rambled on. "Just you. She lusts after you."

Finn's brows drew inward. This guy really was crazy. Addie didn't mention anything about him, and he wondered if Aaron had ever approached her. "Let my sister go. This is between you and me."

"No." He shook his head violently, bringing the knife up. "No. I'm going to kill her."

"No!" Finn roared, jumping across the room as Aaron brought the knife down.

A gunshot tore through the air behind him and Aaron jerked back. The knife dropped on Kelsey's side, nicking her. She screamed, long and loud, as Aaron's body fell to the floor beside the bed.

Finn rushed to her, trying to undo the knots at her wrists with shaking hands. Finally he picked up the knife and cut through the rope at her wrists and ankles. She shot up, crushing him in a hug, shaking against him. "It's okay, you're okay," He murmured into her hair as he rocked her. He repeated it over and over, trying to convince them both.

"Finn, we need to examine her. The paramedics are close." Krakowski touched Finn's shoulder.

Finn nodded, not wanting to let her go yet. Jesus Christ, he wouldn't have survived watching her die, too. When he heard the ambulance sirens, he picked Kelsey up, cradling her to his chest, and made his way down the stairs. The officers came behind him.

The paramedics turned the lights on and he followed them to the ambulance. His legs were weak but he made it until he laid her on the stretcher, then he sank down on the edge of the ambulance and heaved in a deep breath.

Krakowski watched him for a minute before speaking. "What you did was reckless and stupid."

Finn shot him a dark glare.

"I'm not going to press charges for impeding an investigation and your sister is okay. We're going to have to get her statement though, and yours, about what happened in there." Krakowski's face softened. "She's very lucky to have a brother like you."

Finn nodded. He couldn't manage much more now that the adrenaline had worn off and shock replaced it. He still couldn't understand why Aaron had hated him, had been jealous of him and the sick, twisted crush Aaron had on Addie. When he saw her, he'd have to question Addie and see if she'd ever run into him.

Krakowski took their statements, Kelsey's taking longer since she had to pause every few seconds to get the words out. They'd given her something to calm her down, but the fear was still clear in her eyes. Finn couldn't stand to see her like that.

When they finished, Finn rode to the hospital, Kelsey's hand grasping his tight. He brushed her hair back and kissed her forehead. She was going to have trouble with this, but he'd be there to help her through it.

Chapter Thirty-One

Addie

Having Jenna in her apartment was really, really weird. Thank God Gemma was there, or it would've been unbearable. Gemma served as a barrier, getting Jenna a glass of wine while Addie grabbed her a blanket to ward off the chill of shock. Seeing the girl sitting on her couch made Addie feel like she was betraying Halle in the worst way, but she couldn't just leave her there. She owed Finn that much at least.

Her phone chimed and she snatched it off the bar. It was a text from Finn.

Finn: Kelsey safe, at hospital. Do you know where Jenna is?

Relief rushed over her in wave after wave and she sank onto a stool at the bar. Thank God they were both safe.

Addie: She's here with me. Do you want me to bring her up there?

Finn: Please. Thank you for taking care of her. I know how hard that had to be.

Addie: YW. See you in a bit. Gemma will be with me.

"Kelsey and Finn are at the hospital," Addie announced. Gemma and Jenna both looked at her. "I'm going to take you up there. He said that they are both fine, but Kelsey has some injuries the doctor needs to look at."

They climbed back into her car and this time she headed toward the hospital. She wanted to rush to Finn and make sure he was truly okay. Her heart wouldn't settle down until she did.

She parked quickly, if a little recklessly, in the vast lot of the hospital. They got out, each running to the entrance. This night had been beyond weird, with Kelsey being kidnapped and her taking care of Jenna. It was like another freaking dimension, where everything was turned upside down.

They entered the hospital.

"Addie."

She sighed as she turned and saw Halle running toward her.

Halle faltered when she saw Jenna, then straightened her shoulders. "I saw Finn come in with his sister. I'll take you up to her room, the doctor's looking her over now."

Addie put an arm through Halle's as they walked to the elevators. An already awkward situation just got down right unbearable, even with Gemma there. Halle squeezed her hand, looking at her with understanding, and Addie's stomach settled a little. The elevator came fast and they stepped on. Addie and Gemma made sure to stand in between Jenna and Halle. For Jenna's part, she huddled into the hoodie Addie had loaned her and kept her eyes straight ahead.

Halle led them down the hall on the fifth floor. Addie remembered coming up here, heart in throat, when Helena was in the car accident with her friend. She didn't feel that different now, and that made her pause. Did she feel the same about Finn that she did about Helena? As in love?

Addie stopped in the middle of the hallway.

Halle noticed and looked back at her. "Addie?"

She swallowed, catching up to her sister. When Halle raised her brows, Addie shook her head. Now wasn't the time to talk about her realization.

Halle knocked on room 545.

"Come in." Finn's rough voice called.

Her heart thudded in her chest, but she let Jenna go in before her. Addie saw Kelsey first, lying in the hospital bed, face as pale as her blonde hair. Her eyes darted around the room and then settled on Addie and Jenna.

"I'm going to wait in the hall." Gemma whispered to Addie, then stepped outside with Halle.

Addie nodded, her eyes locked on Finn. He sat next to his sister, face haggard, eyes tired. Addie's heart went out to him. She stood by the door, unsure if she had a place in this family reunion.

Jenna rushed to the bed and hugged Kelsey tight. "God, Kelsey. I'm so sorry I wasn't there." She sobbed, arms wrapping tighter.

"It's okay. There was nothing you could do." Kelsey stroked her sister's hair. "He may have hurt you, too."

Jenna kept sobbing. Finn placed a hand on her back and Addie really felt awkward. She turned to go.

"Addie?"

Her hand gripped the doorknob but stopped at the sound of his voice.

"Please, stay." His words, the despair, crashed into her.

She spun around and walked toward him. He moved his hands from Jenna and Kelsey and wrapped his arms around her as she pulled him close. "I was so worried about you," she said into his hair. His head was pressed against her heart.

"You're heart is beating fast," he said, "Just like mine."

She didn't care that his sisters witnessed this, didn't care that it might be shown as a weakness. He was here and he was alive.

"Thank you for taking care of Jenna for me."

"Sure. I wasn't going to leave her there alone." Addie moved back, looked over at his sisters. "Hi, Kelsey. It's nice to meet you."

Kelsey smiled at her, and it lit up her face. She almost looked rejuvenated. "I've heard so much about you."

"Ha, all bad?" Addie winked at Finn.

Kelsey laughed, then winced. "Sorry, hurts to laugh."

Finn cast a worried look over her.

"I'm fine, honestly. Just sore. I'm just glad you were there to save me." She touched Finn's cheek. "Big brother to the rescue."

Addie stood at Finn's side, letting her love for him wash over her, eroding all her reasons that she wanted to stay out of a relationship. This was the man for her, and God help him, he wasn't getting rid of her.

"When are they letting you go?" Jenna sat on the edge of the hospital bed, her hand covering Kelsey's.

"They said they wanted to watch me overnight. Make sure nothing else is wrong, but that I can most likely go home in the morning. Addie, your sister is my nurse tonight. She's been so helpful. I've never met a sweeter person."

Addie wasn't sure, but she thought she saw Jenna flinch when Kelsey said it. "She is. You couldn't be in better hands."

They stayed for a little longer, until the medicine had Kelsey falling asleep. Jenna glanced over at her brother and Addie. "I'll stay with her. You should go home with Addie."

"I can stay, Jenna."

Jenna waved a hand at him. "I'm sure Addie was worried about you, too. Kelsey's just going to sleep, and I'd rather be here than at home alone."

Finn was silent for a minute, then said, "Okay. I'll pick the two of you up in the morning. Just call me, okay? If you need anything."

"I will." She smiled at Addie. "I want to thank you, too. I know that what I did to your sister was wrong, and I can't do enough to make that up to her. That you took me into your home, even with what I did, says so much about you and your family."

Addie nodded, not trusting herself to speak. She wasn't sure that she should forgive Jenna, even after that pretty speech. She'd have to warn Halle that Jenna was staying with Kelsey.

Finn kissed both his sisters on the cheek, repeated that Jenna needed to call him if they needed anything. Halle stood by the nurses' station, speaking with Gemma in soft tones.

"Jenna is going to stay with Kelsey," Addie warned her sister.

Halle nodded, a bleak look on her face. But being the person she was, she'd be professional.

"Carter, Caleb, and the Chief are down the hall with Nate and Noah. We should drop in and say hey," Gemma told them.

"That's a good idea," Addie said, even though she was about to pass out with exhaustion. Tomorrow she was going to sleep for hours.

Chief waved them into the room that held both Noah and Nate. An older woman stood in between their beds, worry plain on her face.

Carter put an arm around Gemma's waist and she leaned into him.

"Are they okay?" Finn asked.

"Yes," the Chief swallowed. "Aaron hit them both on the head with a flashlight. They both have concussions but will be fine."

Finn sighed beside her and Addie knew he was blaming himself for this.

"Aaron never showed any signs of this, but I should've seen it." Chief rubbed a hand down his face. His shoulders drooped.

"It's no one's fault but Aaron's. He was crazy." Addie spoke softly. "There was nothing anyone could've done."

Chapter Thirty-Two

Finn

The evening ran through his mind as he drove. Addie had taken him to get his truck from the fire house, and they headed to her apartment. His body ached and exhaustion had settled in, and he forced his eyes to stay open as he drove. What Aaron said kept turning over and over in his mind, and when he woke up in the morning, he'd have to ask Addie about it.

They both took the stairs to her apartment slowly and made it inside. Harlow meowed crazily until Addie picked her up. Neither was awake enough for a shower, so they collapsed on the bed, Harlow winding between them. Finally, at four in the morning, they were ready to sink into sleep.

Finn pulled Addie to him, his chest to her back, and sighed into her hair. She settled against him, matching her breathing to his. Harlow curled up in a ball at their knees, nuzzling his legs. Now that his sister was safe, Finn focused on Addie. On the feel of her curled into him, of her smell and the sound of her breathing.

"Finn?" Addie spoke sleepily.

"Yeah?"

"I love you."

He stiffened, a wave of shock hitting him. A slow smile spread across his face. "Thank God."

"Thank God?" She shifted to look at him in the near darkness. "Wow."

He laughed softly, hoping she could see his smile. "I was wondering how long I was going to have to fight for that." He nuzzled her neck, kissed up to her jaw. "I love you, too."

She sighed happily. "Thank God."

They both fell asleep, smiling, relaxed against each other.

§§

Finn woke up first the next day, the sun glaring into the room, and glanced at his phone. It was 1:00pm. He shot up in the bed, seeing that he'd missed a call from Jenna. He dialed her number fast.

"Hey, sleepyhead." Jenna sang into the phone.

"I didn't mean to sleep this long." He saw Addie shift beside him. She looked up at him questioningly. He mouthed 'Jenna' and she nodded.

"It's okay. Trevor brought me my car this morning, and I took Kelsey home. She's passed out right now. Carter, Gemma, Caleb and Autumn cleaned up the house this morning before we got home. All we have to do is paint the wall where the bastard put the tattoo up."

"I'll be over in a few minutes." He moved to get off the bed.

"No, Finn. Honestly, she's going to sleep a while and I'm ready to crash. Trevor is here, and I made sure all the doors are locked," Jenna told him.

Didn't Jenna understand that having Trevor there didn't make Finn feel like they were any safer? "Jenna, I can come over."

"Finn, stop. You need a day off, some rest. I'm going to take care of Kelsey. I owe her that for not being there, okay? You did your rescuing last night. It's my turn."

He sighed, "Fine. Damn it. But call me if you need me. I mean it."

"I will, big brother."

He heard the smile in her voice and hung up, lying back

down beside Addie. Her eyes were still slumberous as she smiled at him.

"She wants you to stay." She leaned closer.

"Yeah, Kelsey's asleep anyway and Trevor's there. Although, that doesn't make me happy." He trailed a hand down her arm.

"I understand that. He cheated a ton, but was never physically violent toward Halle, so your sister is safe from that part." Addie pressed a kiss to his lips, sinking into his arms.

"Hmm, I think we may need a shower." Finn spoke against her lips. "We both stink."

She hit him in the arm, laughing, before she slid out of the bed. "And I'm starving. We can go get something to eat when we're done." She waggled her eyebrows at him and he followed her into the bathroom.

He took his time in the shower, washing her hair and body, pressing tender kisses along her skin. He wanted to show her how much she meant to him, to prove how deep he loved her. Her expression mirrored his own and his heart swelled. Love like this was something he'd thought was a myth. But it existed, with her. Their touches became more urgent, more heated, until they were moving together, hot and slick.

After their shower, they dressed comfortably and headed to his truck. The weather was cool, but bright, a direct opposite from the events of last night. He tried not to let it darken his thoughts and focused on Addie instead. On her finally admitting that she loved him. It was freedom to admit the same thing to her. He just didn't know where they went from here.

They picked a fast food restaurant, grabbing burgers, drinks, and fries, before heading back to the apartment. Addie fed Harlow while Finn placed everything out on the bar.

"You know, we need to look at a place where we actually have a kitchen table," he murmured around the burger.

Addie jumped beside him, mouth open. "Wha-?"

"Close your mouth." He nonchalantly bit into his burger, chewed, and swallowed. She stared at him until he spoke again. "It makes sense."

"It does, does it?" Her lips twitched and he guessed the shock passed. "We're just going to move in together? Just like that?"

"Sure." Finn grinned. "Don't you want to?"

"I still have six months left on my lease." She watched him closely.

"Good, it'll take us at least that long to find the right house." Finn's face turned serious. "But only if this is what you want. I don't want you to do it unless you're absolutely sure."

Addie bit her lip and he could tell she thought about it. Then she leaned in and kissed him soundly. "We can start looking tomorrow."

He was finally happy, he thought as he finished eating. He'd met an awesome, strong, fiery woman that filled the empty spaces inside of him. Hopefully Isaac was looking down on him and was content with the choices he'd made. He wanted Isaac to be happy wherever he was and know that Finn was doing whatever possible to protect Kelsey.

His thoughts did turn dark at that. Aaron had always seemed like a good guy. Wanting to help the community, working hard. He'd never once got the vibe from Aaron that he hated him. Or was jealous.

That reminded him, he needed to call Jack and let him know what happened, and that he'd found the arsonist. It still surprised him that it wasn't someone from his military past. Maybe Aaron had paid more attention to his tattoo than he thought.

"Hey, you're getting that frown again." Addie waved her hand in front of his face.

He blinked, mustered up a smile. "Sorry, just confused about Aaron."

"I know. But what happened with him wasn't your fault. It was his." She stood and started putting trash in the brown burger bag. "There was just something messed up in his head, and for some reason he targeted you. And Kelsey. But now he's dead and it's over."

Finn really hoped it was. According to the evidence, it was over. He just had to accept that. Kelsey was safe, and Aaron was dead. "You're right. It's over."

"Good. There's that smile." She leaned over the bar and gave him another kiss.

Chapter Thirty-Three

Addie

Chaos reigned in her classroom as the kids twirled and jumped in their costumes. It was Halloween, a Friday, and the kids were hyped up on sugar and soda. She'd already taken the maximum dose of Excedrin, and even though her headache throbbed, she enjoyed watching the kids have fun.

She, Gemma, and Autumn had stayed late last night to decorate each of the classrooms. It gave her something to do, since Finn had a shift at the station anyway. God, she was already thinking of them as a couple. Which, they were, but it was how easy she thought of them that way that shocked her. She'd always been against relationships, against trusting someone on that level, but Finn showed her that she could.

A group of girls shrieked. She looked at them and saw that one of the boys had thrown a fake spider into the mix.

The girls danced around, waving their hands, dramatic even though by now they knew it was fake. She smiled to herself at how easy life had been at that age.

Since Finn had a shift tonight, she was going to pass candy out at her apartment. Plenty of kids in her apartment complex dressed up and she loved the look on their faces when she dropped the candy in their bags.

When the bell finally, mercifully rang, the kids flew out of the classroom, bags of candy and book bags on their arms. Autumn entered the classroom a minute later.

"Tell me again why it's illegal to imbibe alcohol at work." She sank into one of the chairs and rubbed her forehead.

"I can't think of a reason right now." Addie grinned at her friend. "Are you and Caleb doing anything tonight?"

"I think so."

"That sounded enthusiastic." Addie peered at her friend, trying to discern what bothered her.

"Ugh." Autumn slumped in the chair. "He wants me to meet his parents again."

"Why is that such a problem?" Addie was genuinely curious. Now that she and Finn had cemented their relationship, she wondered how meeting his parents would be. It couldn't be as bad as finding out Jenna was his sister.

"It's seems so final and I'm not sure I want this to be final." Autumn leaned on her elbow and looked at Addie. "I see Gemma and Carter, and now you and Finn, and I can't help but wonder if fate is against me. That Caleb will be the one I end up with."

Addie wanted to laugh it off. The idea had some merit, but she wasn't going to tell Autumn that. "I think that you should just go with the flow, let things happen."

"When did you become a Zen master?" Autumn rolled her eyes, then sighed. "Damn it, you're right though. All I'm doing is making myself miserable thinking about this."

"Exactly. So stop worrying and have fun." Addie realized what she said could apply to herself, too. "I hate being right."

Autumn laughed, her eyes sparkling. "Yep."

On the way home Addie thought about swinging by the firehouse to surprise Finn but wasn't sure if that was an okay thing to do yet or not. She decided against it, not wanting to upset him. She was still a little unsteady with this relationship stuff and didn't want to ruin it before it really began. It took her a bit longer than normal to get home, everyone was getting off of work early to get ready for trick-or-treating or Halloween parties.

This was the first year she hadn't gone to one. Without

Finn beside her, she just didn't feel like going. Was she losing her party girl side? Was she being domesticated? She laughed at that as she finally pulled into her apartment complex.

Tonight she'd have to put Harlow up. She didn't want her racing out of the apartment every time she opened the door to pass out candy. She cradled the now not-so-kitten size Harlow and stroked beneath her chin. Harlow purred and nuzzled Addie's neck. Addie's heart warmed at the fact that Finn had thought of her when he'd first seen Harlow. Even then she'd been on his mind.

Even then he'd been on *her* mind.

After setting Harlow down, she found a large, blue Tupperware bowl and set it on the counter. She dumped several bags of Reese's, Butterfingers, and Dots into it, then she set it on the table by the door and went to change into her comfy clothes.

It wouldn't be long before the kids came knocking. She'd thought briefly about dressing up, but the only costumes she had on hand were too sluttish for little ones. Parents would revolt if she wore any of those short-skirted, cleavage-showing clothes. The best thing to do was to stay in her comfy clothes.

The first kid knocked on the door half an hour later. A

tiny Ironman stood before her and his grin showed his front two teeth missing. She heard a few other kids coming up the stairs as she put a handful of candy into his orange bag.

"Thanks." The tiny Ironman spun around and dashed to the next door.

A sweet fairy princess with golden curls and a G.I. Joe with a camo-painted face stepped onto the landing. They whispered furiously to each other about something, but brightened when they saw Addie still standing with her door open.

"Hi," Addie said as they came closer. "You look so pretty."

"Thank you." The girl twirled, her dress sparkling when it caught the light from Addie's apartment.

"And you look very brave," Addie told the boy.

The boy nodded, keeping with the seriousness of the costume.

Addie gave them each handfuls of candy and smiled. They thanked her and ran to the next door.

Kids knocked on her door sporadically. They liked to wait until right when she sat down and she had to giggle at that. Harlow meowed pitifully from her small crate and guilt pinched at Addie. As soon as the kids were done, she'd let Harlow out to play.

She couldn't help but wonder if Finn was thinking of her as he worked at the fire house. God knows she couldn't stop thinking about him. It was ridiculous how easy she'd slid into this. Into thinking about him freely and like a boyfriend.

Once the kids didn't come for at least an hour, Addie let Harlow out. Harlow pranced around, shooting dirty looks at Addie, before deciding to forgive her and rubbed against Addie's legs, purring.

To keep herself occupied and make sure she didn't text Finn every five seconds, she turned on the TV and watched mindless reality shows. The episodes blurred in front of her eyes.

She didn't realize she'd fallen asleep until the knock on her door woke her up. Her first thought was that Finn had gotten off early, so she scrambled up and went to open it.

It wasn't Finn, though, but the girl that had spoken to her when Addie was leaving Jenna's house, Jenna in tow. Addie opened her mouth to ask what she was doing here, when the woman lifted her arm and something pinched the side of Addie's neck. She fell to the floor.

Chapter Thirty-Four

Finn

His shift on Halloween night had been anything but quiet. Kids and people who weren't paying attention had caused both the police and the fire department a lot of trouble. But now the only thing on his mind was seeing Addie, getting some food, and taking a shower to wash away the grime.

The stairs to the second level of the apartments seemed like a formidable opponent, but Addie waited, so he took them two at a time, the muscles in his legs screaming. He figured she'd fallen asleep since she hadn't answered his texts in a while, so he'd knock quietly.

The dark landing sent a chill through his body. He dismissed it, the light probably went out again. When he reached Addie's door and saw that it was slightly ajar, the chill went to his bones. Something was wrong, and Addie was involved. For a moment his brain stuttered as a fear previously unknown slammed into him. He'd feared when Kelsey was kidnapped, but this was a whole new animal.

He took a deep breath, telling himself that Addie may have forgotten to shut the door. The lights were on inside, and he surveyed the room. No signs of a struggle. Nothing out of place. The TV was on in the small living room and Harlow pounced into the room when she heard him swear. She gave a pitiful meow and Finn reached down to pet her one time.

"Where's Addie?" Finn whispered to the cat as he stood back up. He checked the kitchen, bathroom, and her bedroom, calling her name loud enough that the neighbors probably heard. It looked like she just stepped out, but when he saw her purse and keys on the bar and her cell phone on the couch, his stomach dropped. She'd never leave without those. No woman would.

He grabbed her cell phone and checked to see if she'd seen any of his texts. When the screen showed that they were all unopened, he had a roundabout time that she was taken. He knew she wouldn't leave on her own.

The first thing he had to do was alert the police and call the firehouse. Chief and Carter needed to know. Then he'd call Nick and Luke and let them know. He dreaded that call. Those men were very protective of their new sister and would be highly pissed that something had happened.

Did some crazy man take her from the apartment? Had he dressed up so no one could see them? How did he get out of here without anyone spotting them?

That gave him an idea. He'd check with the neighbors.

He turned to go back outside and jerked to a stop. His fists clenched and his body went cold. On the inside of Addie's door someone had carved his tattoo. Holy shit. So it wasn't over.

He went to Addie's next door neighbor and knocked as loudly as he could. It took a minute and he rocked on his heels and thrummed his fingers on the door jam before he heard the door unlock. A woman in sweats and a t-shirt hesitantly cracked the door.

"Yes?" She peered through.

"Hi. I'm sorry to bother you so early." Finn stood back from the door to show the lady he wasn't trying to harm her.

She saw the Sanctuary Bay Fire Department shirt he wore and relaxed a little.

"Your next door neighbor, Addie, is my…girlfriend. I just got here and her door was open, her TV on and her phone, purse, and car are still here. I wanted to know if you saw anything?" He wasn't going to mention the tattoo carved into the door.

"No, I've been asleep, and so has my family," she told him. "Check with everyone else and see."

Finn nodded as she shut the door quietly, then took his phone out and called the Chief. The Chief hated hearing that Addie was missing and said he'd relay the message to Carter and Caleb. After he ended that call, and after he spoke with Nick and Luke, he called the detective assigned--or was assigned, since the case was supposedly dead--and told him what he'd found. Krakowski swore into the phone and told Finn to stay there and not touch anything until he got there.

Since he couldn't touch anything, and his body was urging him to do something--anything--he went around the apartment complex to talk to the other residents. Each door opened with the same news. No one had seen or heard anything. Was the freaking person that took Addie a damn ghost? How could nobody see or hear anything? Addie would've fought like a hellcat to keep from being taken.

An unbidden thought rose in his head, that Addie was an accomplice and not a victim, but he squashed it quickly. Addie would never do something like that and right now she needed him. Needed him to find her whole and alive.

The detective didn't take long to get there. He arrived

with two coffees in hand, in jeans and a button up instead of his usual suit. It looked like Finn had woken him, but he couldn't find the heart to care. The detective held out the coffee and when Finn first refused he held it out longer. "We're going to need you at the top of your game, Sergeant Thompson."

Finn knew Krakowski had looked into his past and would've seen the time he served in the Marines. Giving in, he took the coffee and downed it in three gulps. "Satisfied?"

Krakowski nodded. "I thought that Aaron died the night he had your sister."

Finn's eyes glinted. "Someone else must've been in on it. No one else knows about the symbols except people I trust."

"You trusted Aaron."

Finn stepped into Addie's apartment, waited for Krakowski to step in, and shut the door. "No, not like I trust everyone else."

Krakowski accepted the answer and stared at the back of the door. Then he turned and surveyed the apartment. "You didn't touch anything?"

"Nothing but the cat," Finn said. "Harlow," he clarified when Krakowski raised his brows.

"There's no one else you can think of that would be in league with Aaron? That would want to finish this?" Krakowski stared at Finn. "Because for someone to do this…they have to have a pretty deep hatred of you."

"I don't know." Finn wrestled with the thought, shoving his hands through his hair. Everything shifted, uneven under his feet and he knew that if he didn't save Addie, nothing would be stable again. "I've only known Aaron since I moved here. I don't think he could've developed a reason to hate me that much. Plus, he came here before me by several months."

"That doesn't make much sense. There has to be a connection between you and Aaron. I think that's the angle we need to consider, to pursue. Can you get your Sergeant-Major to get his FBI friend to help?"

"They're going to have to."

"Why don't you call him, and I'll call her family and notify them." Krakowski put a hand on Finn's shoulder, compassion in his eyes. "We'll get her back."

Finn jerked his head in answer, then stepped outside to call Jack. If he got to the person first and there was a single bruise or scratch on Addie, he'd kill them.

Chapter Thirty-Five

Addie

She woke, groggy and sore, to find herself in a darkened room. The smell of mildew and wet wood permeated the area and she gagged into the piece of cloth covering her mouth. When she tried to pull the gag out, her arms wouldn't move. Something hard cut into her wrists, and her arms were tied behind her back to the wooden chair.

Fear threatened to overwhelm her but she forced it back with anger and curiosity. Who the hell kidnapped her and why the hell did they bring her to wherever this was? Vaguely, through the fog in her mind, she remembered answering the door. But the harder she concentrated, the more piercing the headache became.

She strained to hear if someone was nearby but all she heard was the steady drip, drip, drip of water somewhere in the room. Her imagination flared to life, coming up with a myriad of scenarios where she died painfully.

It felt like hours, maybe days, as she sat in the darkness, struggling against the rough zip ties. Her ankles and wrists burned from the movement and she wore herself out, breathing raggedly. The grogginess was beginning to dissipate and so was her headache, so maybe she could focus better.

Now she remembered the woman who'd been at Kelsey and Jenna's house and who'd knocked on her door last night. At least, she thought it was last night. Time had no meaning in the darkness of wherever she was. The woman was impossibly beautiful, a model's willowy body and chestnut colored hair. Hazel eyes that went from sweet to hard in the moment Addie opened the door. She remembered the pinch in her neck and realized the woman had drugged her. How else would she have gotten Addie to go peacefully and quietly with her?

Addie stopped struggling against the ties, giving her hands and ankles rest and focused her eyes in the darkness. She could see the silhouette of pipes and cement walls. A door looked to be directly in front of her, maybe twenty feet away, and the drip was still steady. It would drive her into insanity if she kept focusing on the sound.

A little while later, Addie's eyes jerked open at the

sound of a latch being forced open. She sat up as straight as she was able, her eyes narrowed in the direction of the door. A light blazed on, blinding her for a second and the sound of high heels on cement floor moved in her direction.

Once Addie blinked and her eyes adjusted, she saw the woman. She started to talk around the gag.

"Hush. I'll take it off." The woman sashayed around the chair and undid the gag, letting it fall around Addie's neck.

"Who the hell are you?" Addie spit out the nasty taste of the gag. "Why did you kidnap me?"

"My name is Mia." The woman grabbed a chair in the corner and sat in front of Addie. "You have something that is mine."

Addie quirked a brow. "Really? And what might that be?"

Mia crossed her never ending legs and smiled, baring her teeth. "Finn."

Addie's heart went into overdrive. What did she want with him? Was Finn okay? Damn it, she needed to get out of these stupid restraints. "Stay the fuck away from him!"

Mia laughed, husky and beautiful, but the sound grated on Addie's nerves. "Like you can do anything right now. Besides, Finn has always loved me."

"Yeah, he must've loved you so much that he came to

me. Told me he wanted to move in with me, love me. Did he ever do that for you?"

Mia backhanded her and Addie's head jerked to the side. Her eyes were manic as she held Addie's cheeks in a vice like grip. "He has only loved me. Me! I gave him time to grieve for his stupid friend, and let him move here. I am what he needs, and will be the only one he loves. Not his fucking sisters, not you." She roughly let go and took a deep breath.

Addie watched the transformation with wide eyes. One minute the bitch was crazy, the other calm. No wonder Finn was hesitant to get into a relationship with someone else. Addie's stomach clenched. She wouldn't let this crazy hooker near him again. She just had to find a way out of this.

"It would've worked out perfectly if Aaron did his part. But no, he had to get caught, had to get himself shot. At least I don't have to put up with his roaming hands anymore." Mia sighed. "He was my stepbrother, a long time ago. He was easy to seduce, easy to get him to work with me. To hate Finn. Anything to get me to sleep with him."

Addie shut her eyes against the hate rolling off of this woman. She said she loved Finn, but wanted to hurt him any way she could. Didn't she know that definitely wasn't love? That it was twisted and depraved? And her stepbrother? Wasn't there some unspoken rule about sleeping with a step-anything?

"I knew that Finn would eventually move near his sisters here, so I had Aaron get a job with the fire department. I didn't expect Finn to join the fire department, so that was a nice surprise." Mia pursed red covered lips. "I didn't count on him getting to know *you*."

Addie shuddered at the venom in that one word. For the first time real fear consumed her. This crazy bitch saw Addie as a roadblock in her delusion of getting Finn all to herself. There had to be some way that she could get out of here, if not whole, then alive.

"Soon it won't matter, you'll be dead and no one will stand in my way." The nonchalant way Mia said it freaked Addie out more than if she'd screamed it in her face.

Mia stepped forward and Addie only just stopped herself from flinching. The psycho didn't seem to notice, only jerked the gag into place with hard movements. Mia turned back to the door, flicking the light off as she left, plunging Addie back into darkness.

Jesus Christ, how did she get into this situation? Addie's shoulders sagged. She couldn't get out of the restraints, they were too tight, and she wondered if anyone knew she was missing yet. There was no way to tell time, so she had no idea if it'd been a few days or a few hours. God, she wanted to go home, wanted to see her sisters, her nieces, her parents. Wanted to kiss Finn and have him hold her.

The dripping seemed to get louder with each passing minute. Fire spread on the nerves of her hands and feet and numbness through her feet and legs. Her butt and lower back ached from sitting in one position in the hard chair for so long. She knew if she could get out of the chair she could take the bitch down, but getting out of the zip ties seemed impossible.

As her eyes adjusted to the darkness again she tried to see if there was anything she could do to get out of this. Mia had made sure there was nothing in the bare cement room for Addie to use. As far as Addie could tell, she was fucked.

Chapter Thirty-Six

Finn

He knew he drove everyone crazy with his pacing, but if he sat still he might explode. Addie's family and friends gathered in Victoria's living room, all following his movements. Nick and Luke had identical expressions of fury and worry, and Addie's family all looked sick.

How had he allowed it to happen? Had he put Addie in danger by becoming closer to him? From finally opening up and *living*, did he cause her death? He cursed and looked out the window, staring at nothing in the darkness. He didn't cause this. He couldn't blame himself for this.

Sergeant-Major and the FBI agent were searching for a connection between Aaron and Finn. Detective Krakowski was in the kitchen, talking low and furious. He fucking hoped something broke soon. The thought of Addie scared and hurt raked agony through him.

"Finn, would you like some coffee?" Halle stopped

beside him, a steaming mug in her hand.

He looked at her and saw the expression on her face. It stopped him from snapping. "I look that bad?"

The smile didn't reach her eyes. "I think we all do." She pressed the mug into his hands.

Luke's and Nick's stares burned into his back. He didn't blame him, even though he knew they couldn't make him feel any more guilty than he already did. The waiting was shredding his emotions. He *had* to find Addie soon.

Questions swam in Halle's eyes but he saw she held them back with an iron will. After explaining for the fiftieth time what happened when he'd gotten off this morning, Addie's family had finally subsided with the questions. Nothing new had come to light and he hated it. Hating waiting, wondering what was happening to her.

His fingers curled in on his palm, and the pain from his nails cutting into his skin centered him a little. Facing losing Addie was dredging up memories of Isaac dying. It was almost too much but he knew he had to hold on for Addie.

When his cell rang on a nearby table he snatched it off and answered it.

"We've got a connection, but it's faint. I'm not sure it's much to go on." Sergeant-Major's voice came over the line.

"Tell me." Finn's fingers tightened around the phone.

"Aaron had a step-sister about ten years ago. By the name of Mia Hanna."

Ice cold fingers of dread slid down Finn's spine. He couldn't process what he'd just heard, even though he wasn't surprised that Mia would pull something like this.

"Son? Did you hear me?"

"Yeah." Finn cleared his throat. "Do you have an idea where she is?"

"We're looking now. It shouldn't be long."

He hung up the phone and ran a shaking hand through his hair. Fuck, fuck, fuck. He'd known Mia was crazy but murder had seemed out of her league. But if she was attacking his sister and Addie, that meant she wanted to see him. She would have to give him a clue to do that. What was he missing?

"What did he say?" Krakowski moved into the living room. Deep blue circles sat under his eyes and fatigue lined his mouth.

"It's my fucking ex-girlfriend, Mia." Finn spit out. He shot a look of apology toward Victoria and her girls, but Victoria waved it off.

"Where is she?" Nick stood from the couch, Luke following a second later. Both were as tense as Finn, and he knew that if he had to go find Mia, they were coming with him. The detective would just have to face it, none of them were staying behind. There was no telling if Mia had other guys seduced into doing her bidding, and he'd need their MMA training. Knowing he wasn't going to face this alone gave him more confidence, a steadiness he desperately needed.

"They don't know yet. But she wouldn't do all this without wanting to see me, to show me that she was doing this. In her twisted mind, she's making sure we'll be together and that I know it's her. There's a clue somewhere that I'm missing, I just don't know what it means."

"Psychopaths usually go to a place that has some deeper meaning to them. If she's focusing on you, it could be somewhere meaningful to the two of you."

Finn turned at the soft spoken voice and saw Helena sitting on the couch, cheeks red. He walked over and crouched down in front of her. "They do?"

She nodded shyly. "I'm taking psychology and I'm interested in Criminology. I've been studying."

"Thank you." Finn took her hand in his and said it with all the thankfulness he could. He stood, racking his brain to figure out what place could be meaningful for them. This time they let him pace unheeded, and he let the memories of his time with Mia flood his mind. There was so much, it had been quick and heated, but there had to be another connection.

"What about the tattoo?" Krakowski asked. "Maybe it wasn't just to get your attention."

"She was with us when we got it. It was in an old warehouse that the owner had redone to fit his business. But how does that help?" Finn stared at the group, barely holding on to his temper. He wanted to find Addie now.

"There are four abandoned warehouses in the farm country south of Sanctuary Bay. I inspected them a few years back for a client. Wanted to know if I would work for them, redo it." Addie's dad told them. "If that's the connection, that's where they would be."

"I say we go now," Luke said. "There's four of us, we can search them and find the bitch."

"Let's go." Finn grabbed his phone and keys without looking back. He got in his truck and Luke slid into the passenger seat.

"We're going in pairs. Krakowski said it would be safer. We'll each search two of the properties. Wes is texting us the addresses." Luke buckled his seat belt. "Go."

Finn didn't waste any more time. In his rearview mirror he saw Nick and Krakowski in the police car behind him.

He slowed down, letting Krakowski pass. A few seconds later the siren and lights came on and Finn sped up. His hands shook around the steering wheel and he tried to get control. He had to handle this, had to be at the top of his game to help her. Nothing could happen to her. He wouldn't survive it.

Glancing at the almost-set sun, Finn knew that the longer it took to find Addie, the worse her situation could be. He remembered search and rescue teams in Afghanistan and what they sometimes found. The blood, the headless, the sand.

Fuck.

Chapter Thirty-Seven

Addie

Her mind reeled with the possibilities of what Mia was going to do to her. Mia's voice filtered through the door, and by the answering replies, she had two guys with her. Addie figured her chances of survival had seriously dwindled since the two goons arrived.

Hearing them talk so calmly, voices reasonable, about her being in the chair and apparently in the middle of nowhere, left her spirits flagged. She couldn't face the three by herself. Maybe Mia on her own, but not with a group that size. Nick and Luke had taught her minimal self defense training, but she'd always laughed it off. Sanctuary Bay was a small town with a very low crime rate and she hadn't thought she'd need it.

Playing the waiting game was seriously starting to unravel what little was left of her sanity. When would Mia come back, and would she attack Addie then? Was she really not going to see her family again? Or Finn? Was this her last day of life?

Those questions ripped through her mind and she tried hard not to focus on them. To try and be positive the entire time. She laughed mirthlessly. How could she be positive at a time like this?

Finn would find her. He would. Eventually they would connect Mia to Aaron and from there, he would find her. She just hoped it wasn't after what Mia had planned for her.

The minutes ticked by extra slow. The drip, drip, drip continued, edging her closer to insanity. Musk and mildew scented the air as Addie tried to figure out a way to survive. Damn, she wanted to just move her arms. Her shoulders were past the point of sore and moved toward outright agony.

A few minutes later the latch scraped and the door swung open. Light flooded into the room and then Addie saw Mia standing in front of the two guys. A sour taste swam in her mouth and she shook off the dizziness. She wouldn't let them see how much she dreaded what was going to happen next.

One of the men stepped forward, holding out a switch blade. Addie bit her lip to keep her scream inside. His grin sent cold chills through her. Was this guy going to be a part of her torture? When he leaned over, the smell of body odor and cigarettes hit her, but she ignored it as he first cut the zip ties from her ankles and then moved behind her to cut the ones at her wrists. Addie immediately brought her arms back to her lap and fought the groan at the pain shooting through them.

Mia's twisted smile and the frenzied look in her eyes let Addie know that the pain now was going to be nothing compared to what would happen in a little while. "Bring her, James."

James' sweaty hand wrapped around her upper arm and jerked her up. Addie held back another pain filled gasp and her mind raced with thoughts of escape. Mia and the other guy had already left the room. As James pushed her out the door, Addie's foot caught on the cement threshold. His grip tightened and this time she couldn't hold back the gasp of pain.

"Don't try to escape. It's pointless. Both James and Ronnie know how to cause a girl pain. That's why I hired them." Mia sat on the corner of an old wooden desk centered in the large room.

Addie knew where they were now. An abandoned warehouse outside of Sanctuary Bay. Her shoulders sagged and she lost some of her defiance. No one would think to look here. She was truly on her own.

"Aww, don't lose that fight yet. They're hoping that you've got a spark in you." Mia grinned. "I can't wait to watch."

Watch? Bile rose in Addie's throat but she forced it down. She wasn't going to let Mia know how this affected her.

In the dim lighting Addie could make out a lumpy mattress laid against the far wall. Murky brown stains and a sharp odor covered it. Addie's knees started to shake. This couldn't really be happening.

Mia jerked her head toward the mattress and James hauled Addie to it. She struggled, kicking and hitting at him, but he only laughed at her. The blows were weak since she hadn't ate or drank anything in a while and her head still ached from the drugs.

She tried pretending to faint, becoming dead weight, but James only threw her over his shoulder. Her breath came in short, hard gasps as terror gripped her. She didn't want to die, but she had a feeling she wasn't going to make it out of this.

James dropped her half on the mattress, her knees striking the concrete. She rolled over, sucking in air, reaching for her knees. He grabbed her wrists and pushed them above her head.

No matter how much she wiggled and squirmed, kicked and bit, it just seemed to make James enjoy it more. Over his shoulder Addie could see Mia and Ronnie standing, waiting for their turn to hurt her. Black spots swam in her vision as panic invaded. This couldn't be happening, not really. This was Sanctuary Bay. No crime here. She'd always been safe.

Hard fingers gripped her chin and James crushed his mouth to hers. When she didn't open, he bit down on her lower lip. She cried out and he thrust his tongue into her mouth. She gagged and pushed at his shoulders, desperately trying to get this horror to stop.

She couldn't bring her knees up to hurt him because he laid directly on top of her. His erection pressed into her thigh and the bile rose again. Within a second he had his hands underneath her shirt, searching for her bra. She struggled, not moving him an inch.

Chapter Thirty-Eight

Finn

Frustration and fear fueled him as he stormed out of the first abandoned warehouse he and Luke searched. Nothing, not a damn thing, was inside. The place looked like Finn could nudge it and the whole thing would crash to the dirt and dead grass around it. He and Luke didn't waste any time getting into the truck and speeding out of the drive.

Finn glanced up, saw the moon, and his chest tightened. Were they going to find Addie in time? God, they had to. They fucking had to. It was only a ten minute drive to the next warehouse they needed to search, but to Finn it felt like hours. Like time moved against him, kept him back, like it was on Mia's side.

Luke sat, as tense as he was, and Finn was glad that Luke and Nick looked with him. He fully intended to be with Addie for the rest of his life, and having his future brothers-in-law help look for her made his respect for them skyrocket.

They pulled into the drive of the other warehouse, the tires crunching on the gravel. Finn shut the headlights off and coasted to a stop. Another two cars were parked toward the back. He shot Luke a look. Luke nodded and texted Nick their location.

Finn ran to the door at the far side of the warehouse, Luke on his heels. The door swung open and he stepped inside. Dim lights hung over what looked like an abandoned office and a desk with an ancient computer sitting on the top sat to the side. By the thickness of the layers of dust, the warehouse had been abandoned for a long time.

Someone screamed, *Addie* screamed, and all thoughts fled from Finn's mind.

"Finn, wait. We don't know--"

Finn ignored Luke's warning and then his string of expletives as he rushed through the opposite door into the interior of the warehouse. The lighting was even more dim in here, but it didn't stop Finn from spotting Mia, who stood beside a large man. She looked beautiful but it was surrounded by an air of cruelty that disgusted him. Addie screamed again and his gaze shot past them, seeing her dark hair splayed out on a mattress, another man pawing at her clothes. Pure rage slammed into him and he lost his breath.

"Get off of her, you fucker!" Finn dashed across the concrete floor.

The guy standing by Mia spun around, agile even with his bulky size, and sneered at Finn.

Mia shot Finn a sly smile. "Hello, Finn. I knew you'd find me. That you'd remember this special time between us." Mia waved her hand at him when she saw him watching the guy on top of Addie. "Oh, she'll be out of the way soon, baby."

"Get off of her. Now." Finn's voice was filled with lethal intensity. If that guy didn't do it, he'd fucking murder him.

"Get over her, Finn. She's nothing."

At Mia's words, Finn finally looked at her again. "You're wrong. She's my everything."

Mia's eyes widened, then hardened. "No, she's not. Ronnie, subdue him until James is done with the whore."

Ronnie grinned, his rough face wrinkling. "Sure thing."

Finn needed to get to Addie, now. The thug covering her was making fucking *noises*.

"I've got him." Luke said from behind him.

"Good." Finn moved to the side and Ronnie eyed both

he and Luke warily. Finn knew that Luke could handle himself.

Mia snarled at him but he ignored her. His only thought was to get to Addie.

Once Luke threw a punch and Ronnie covered his face to block it, Finn ran to the mattress. He gripped James' collar and lifted. His muscles strained, the guy was pure muscle, but he didn't let go.

"What the fuck?" James spun around, landing a hit to Finn's jaw.

Finn's head snapped to the side but he didn't stop. He hit James in the gut, knocking the breath out of the guy. James may have been tall and thick, but Finn was fast. He didn't slow down, hitting James over and over, going for his nose, face, and kidneys. Behind him he heard Luke and Ronnie fighting, but blocked it out. The rage he felt wouldn't be satisfied until James was deadweight.

When James landed a few hits of his own, Finn didn't feel them. His adrenaline was shredding through his veins and he let out every ounce of his anger and grief into each hit. Addie had to be safe, be avenged, and so did Kelsey.

"You stupid whore."

Finn heard Mia's venom filled voice and looked around James to see her grabbing Addie by her hair. He took a step, eyes locked on Addie, when James swung at his face. The hit connected with his cheek bone and pain blossomed. He didn't miss the sudden rage that filtered onto Addie's face or the way that Addie grabbed at Mia's legs and pulled her down onto the mattress.

That's my girl.

Knowing that Addie could handle Mia one on one, he focused on putting James down. He kept moving and only stopped when James' eyes rolled back in his head and he slumped to the floor.

"You stupid bitch. One, I'm not a whore." Addie punched Mia in the face as she straddled her on the mattress. "Two, you don't hurt my man's sister." She threw a harder punch. "And three, you don't murder women from my town."

Finn let her have a few more punches and when he heard Nick calling out to them, he pulled her off a listless Mia.

It hurt to draw in breath now that the fight was over. Now that he had Addie back in his arms. He looked at her, saw her messy hair, the blood that trickled from her mouth, the numerous bruises forming on her skin. Her clothes were torn and in disarray but all he really saw was the relief in her dark blue eyes.

"Baby, it's okay." Finn reached a hand underneath her neck and knees and pulled her onto his lap. "They won't ever touch you again." He ran his hands over her, making sure she didn't have any worse injuries. His heart pounded in his chest and his hands tightened on her.

Krakowski handcuffed the two men and Mia, calling for backup and paramedics on his radio. He looked relieved that Addie was found and took a deep breath.

"Thank you." Addie whispered against Finn's chest.

He kissed the top of her head in answer.

"Hey, Addie." Luke knelt down beside Finn and gave Addie a small smile.

Addie nodded toward Luke and Nick. "Thanks, guys."

"You're welcome, sis." Nick's eyes softened when he looked at her. "I'm going to call the family and let them know you're okay."

Finn listened to them talk but only focused on Addie. She was alive, he could feel her chest rise and fall in ragged breaths. Jesus Christ, what if they hadn't gotten there when they did? What had Mia been thinking?

Sirens burst through the night, heralding the arrival of backup and ambulance. The paramedics rushed in after the police and it was hard for Finn to hand Addie over to them. When they took her out, he followed them, not willing to let her out of his sight. He tossed his keys to Luke, walking out into the cool night.

Exhaustion washed over him as the ambulance swayed, driving toward the hospital. He watched as the paramedics did their thing, thinking of Kelsey and Addie and how much they went through because of him. Because of his crazy ex. He hadn't been there to protect them. His past had muddied his relationship with Addie. Would she still want to be with him after this? After Mia?

They took Addie to the ER and put them in a tiny, curtained area. She looked so small in the bed, so fragile. Finn swallowed the lump in his throat and interlaced their fingers.

"I knew you'd come." Addie's eyes cracked open. "I knew you'd figure it out."

"Shh, you need rest." Finn pressed a kiss to her lips. "We can talk when you wake up."

She nodded softly and in the next instant her breathing evened out.

Chapter Thirty-Nine

Addie

When Addie woke up, the first thing she noticed was the pain. Her head pounded, her body was sore, and her cheek hurt like hell. She tried to whisper for Finn, but her mouth was dry. The lights from above seared into her brain and she moved an arm to cover her eyes.

"Addie?" Halle's voice echoed a little, then strengthened. "Here's some ice water." Halle helped her sit up and handed her the Styrofoam cup with a straw.

"Thanks," Addie said after taking a few sips. "Where's Finn?"

"He had to go down the hall to give his statement to the police. Luke and Nick are taking their turn in a minute."

"Hey, you." Victoria grabbed Addie's hand as she stood on the other side of the hospital bed. Her cheeks were tear-stained and her eyes puffy.

"I'm okay." Addie squeezed her hand. "I'm just glad

they found me when they did." Her voice wavered, but she forced the dark thoughts out of her head. She didn't want to think about that right now. She wanted to focus on her family and the fact that James hadn't gotten any further. Tears pricked hot against her eyelids and Addie swallowed a few times to keep them back. Her family looked scared enough as it was and she didn't want to freak them out anymore. "Where are the girls?" An inane question but she needed something normal to focus on.

"Charlotte has them. They're fine, don't worry about them." Victoria pressed a kiss to her cheek. "They can stay as long as we need."

"Are they okay? They're not scared, are they?" Addie struggled to sit up and Halle helped her, placing pillows behind her back.

"No, sweetie. They're just happy you're okay," Victoria told her. "Everyone is."

Addie tried not to let memories of that night flash into her mind. Would Finn think of her differently since all this happened? The thought of him leaving her hurt more than all her physical injuries combined. It didn't surprise her as much as overwhelm. She hadn't thought she was *that* in love with him.

"Baby, are you okay?" Her mother came in, fluttering

nervously, followed by her dad, who was steady and calm.

It steadied her, in turn, having them here. It made her feel more sane. She could push what happened out of her mind. For now that would have to do, she could deal with the emotional scarring later. "I'm good, Mom."

Cecilia kissed her face several times, then leaned back and looked over her. "Do you need anything? A drink, some food, some medicine?"

Addie laughed softly, ignoring the pain that shot through her body. "Mom, I'm okay. I promise." Laughing helped dispel some of the melancholy that hung in the room. Her sisters smiled and her dad even cracked a small grin.

A few minutes later Finn walked in. At the intense look in his eyes, Addie's breathing hitched. He was bloody, dirty, and looked like he'd collapse from exhaustion any minute. That he came to see her caused a warm sensation to start in her chest.

"Can I talk with her for a minute?" Finn looked over the family.

"Sure, sweetie." Cecilia kissed his cheek. "Anything for you."

Wes patted his shoulder on his way out and the sisters followed, leaving Finn and Addie alone.

"Hey." Finn shoved his hands in his blood and dirt caked jeans.

"Hey, yourself." Addie cracked a wobbly smile. Why was it suddenly so awkward?

He stepped next to the bed and looked at her. The way his eyes roamed over her face, the heat in them, warmed her like nothing else could have. The chill of fear and survival lessened until it was gone. She reached out and interlaced their fingers, loving how strong and steady he was.

"I'm sorry this happened. I'm sorry that I wasn't there to protect you." He brought her hand up and kissed the back of it. His lips sent a shock through her and her heart melted at the same time.

"It's not your fault your ex was bat shit crazy. She definitely needs some mental help." Addie leaned her head back to look him in the eyes. He still frowned. "Seriously, Finn. It wasn't your fault. We all thought that it was over, once Aaron died, so how could we anticipate this?"

His jaw clenched. "Damn it, Addie. They could've killed you. Or worse."

At the worse, Addie shuddered. "I know. But you and Nick and Luke found me. *You* saved me from that. Don't beat yourself up."

"I still wish I could've done more. Could've been there that night with you."

"What would she have done then? Just killed me right then and there? You don't know what could've happened if things were different."

"I was so worried," he said. "So worried I wouldn't get there in time. That she was torturing you. I know how I felt when Kelsey was taken, but with you it was entirely different. More of an agony in my soul. Addie, if you hadn't survived, if I hadn't found you, I would've died along with you. I don't know how you did it, but you've slipped behind enemy lines into my heart. I don't think I'll ever get rid of you. I know I don't want to. But, if this has changed how you feel about me, I'll understand. I'll be miserable, but I'll understand."

Addie's eyes misted with tears. She wasn't normally the go-for-the-romance type of girl, but damn it, he'd said such pretty words with such sincere meaning. "I love you, too, you idiot. I'm not going anywhere. This. Wasn't. Your. Fault."

When his lips twitched, her heart lightened. "That's my fighter."

She smiled back. "Now, you were talking about getting a place, right? Because I don't think I can go back to that apartment. It won't feel safe anymore. Oh, God! What about Harlow?"

"She's with the twins and Nick's mom. We have everything covered. All I want you to do is focus on being okay." Finn brushed back her bangs. "I'll look for something after my shift tomorrow. Chief gave me today off."

"That was sweet of him." Addie rubbed her hand over Finn's now infamous tattoo. "I didn't know Isaac, but I think he would be very proud of you, and happy that you met someone as fabulous as me."

He laughed, and she felt weightless. It was a beautiful sound. "He would've loved you."

"Thank you." Addie made sure she poured every once of sincerity and gratitude into that phrase.

"Anytime, fighter." He kissed her softly.

§§

Addie stood on the balcony of her and Finn's new apartment and sighed at the starry night above. Three weeks after the incident she couldn't be happier. Once in a while the nightmares would surface, but Finn would hold her and let her cry it out, or distract her with sexy time.

Waking up next to him every morning or doing the more mundane things like grocery shopping together made each day all the more sweeter.

She really sounded like a romantic now, but being in love did that to a person.

"What are you doing out here?" Finn wrapped his arms around her waist and rested his chin on her shoulder.

"Waiting on you to get home." Addie turned her head and smiled. "How was game night with the guys?"

"Good." He kissed the back of her neck and she shivered. "If I didn't know better, I'd say Luke's in love with Halle. Nick was talking about her and Victoria and Luke's face just lit up."

"Man, it has to be noticeable if you figured that out." She giggled when he nudged her.

"Hey, I have a brand new respect for love now."

"Me too." She sighed, still watching the stars. She never thought she would be this content. It had a weird calming effect on her. She knew it calmed him, too. He had his own nightmares from war, and she did her best to help soothe them. She'd finally talked him into going to a therapist and as he worked with it, he seemed to get a better handle on the PTSD. They both knew it might not ever fully go away, but at least they had ways to deal with it when it surfaced.

"Let's go inside." Finn spun her around, pulling her gently toward the door. "I want to make love to my girlfriend."

She followed, glad she'd been brave enough to take the heat.

Author's Other Works:

The Kismet Series
[Crossing the Line (Book 1)](#)

YA Paranormal Series
[Awakening (The Guardians, #1)](#) free!
[Sacred (The Guardians, #2)](#)

Turn the page to read the first chapter in Crossing the Line

Crossing the Line

Book 1 in The Kismet Series

Chapter One

Victoria stretched to ease the stiffness in her back and looked around the combined living room and kitchen area of the condo. The work made her proud. Color and life, furniture and art now filled the previously hollow room.

Rachel would sell this condo in a flash now.

Her cell rang from inside her purse and she dashed to the bar in the kitchen and dug until she found it. She bit back a curse when she saw the display.

Roger. Roger, who was supposed to be picking up Lucia and Helena from school today. Roger, the ex who wanted to "go find himself" and decided a wife and family weren't part of that. He'd only waited two days after the divorce was finalized to date a socialite.

She reminded herself that the divorce was a year old and that bitterness didn't suit her. "Yes?" If she answered the phone with a little bit of bite in her voice, it didn't make her bitter. It showed how tired she was of him bailing on her.

"Hey, babe." Roger still didn't get the fact that he couldn't call her babe. Ever.

A headache started at the base of her skull. "What is it? I'm busy." She needed to meet her dad and the contractor at her new office.

"I can't pick up the girls from school. I'm having dinner with someone and I'll be late if I don't leave now."

"Roger," she sighed and looked at her watch. The girls needed to be picked up in ten minutes. "You promised me you would get them. Plus, I'm on the other side of town. There's no way I can get there in time." Sanctuary Bay wasn't a large town, but tourist season had started, so traffic would be heavy.

"I'm telling you ahead so that you can make arrangements."

Temper ignited at the exaggerated patience in his voice. "You're telling me ten minutes before they're supposed to be picked up. That's not telling me in advance."

"Look, babe. I can't make it. Give my love to the girls."

Victoria glared at her phone when he hung up. She closed her eyes and took three deep breaths. There was a way to solve this situation without maiming her ex. She'd just have to call one of her sisters.

She dialed her youngest sister, Addison, with her fingers crossed. Addie taught at a school not far from the girls. If there were no meetings, Addie should be able to pick them up.

"Who's my favorite sister?" Her voice dripped syrupy sweet when Addie answered.

"God, what? You only act like this when you need something." Addie said.

Victoria heard the smile in her sister's voice and took heart. "Can you pick up the girls?"

"Did Roger back out again?"

"He decided to have dinner in the city." She leaned against the counter and surveyed the condo again to prove to herself that she'd moved on after the divorce. That she was better off. That her girls were better off.

"That douche. I'll leave right now. But you owe me dinner."

"Thanks, Addie."

After she hung up, she changed into a black pencil skirt, a white button up shirt, and red pumps for the meeting. She pulled her black hair into a sleek ponytail, dressed her brown eyes in natural makeup and mascara.

The drive to the ocean front office on the boardwalk took an extra thirty minutes. It didn't bother her, though, because the warm air smelled like the sea, and she enjoyed every minute of it. She pulled her SUV into the shopping center and spotted her father's truck parked close to the office he'd helped her buy. Being a retired contractor, he recommended a friend of his to redo the inside to fit her needs. She had high hopes on the outcome.

"Hey, sweetie." Her father stood outside the door, his salt and pepper hair close cropped. He shared his sloe eyes with his two eldest daughters, and they warmed when he saw his oldest. "How was the staging?" he enveloped her in a tight hug.

"Great, I finished the condo for Rachel and I have consults tomorrow for a few personal interior designs." Victoria looked at the door. Her stomach tightened in excitement. An office of her own. She wouldn't have to work out of her house anymore. "Let's go in. I want to see it again."

Her father gestured toward her oversized purse. "If you can find the key in that suitcase of yours."

Victoria laughed. "Lucia and Helena bought it for me for my birthday. It's a little big, but they were so excited when I opened it. I think they combined both their allowances for a month to buy it."

"Your mother helped them with some." He said as she pulled the key out.

"See? Only took a minute." With a quick smile she unlocked the door and stepped inside.

Wallpaper hung from the walls in tatters, the carpet smelled musty and had black and red stains all over it. A receptionist counter covered in chipped black and white Formica was the only furniture in the room, thank God, Victoria thought.

"Needs a lot of work."

"I know, Dad. Did I make a mistake? Picking this place out?" Worry clouded her excitement.

"Do you know how you want this place to look?" He looked at her and she saw the faith in his eyes.

She regarded the place and imagined what she wanted. Dark hard wood floors, antique furniture, some potted plants. Graphite colored walls with white trim. Elegance and style. "Definitely."

"Then there's no mistake. You're going to build a business here. You're already doing great out of your house. You'll be able to accommodate more clients out of a real office. You can even get an assistant for scheduling and stuff."

Her father was the driving force behind her confidence. Whenever she couldn't imagine herself with her own business, he built her up. Pushed her toward better things. He looked in the direction of the parking lot at the sound of a truck door shutting. "Here comes Nick now."

Victoria turned when she heard the door to the office open and the shock shot straight to her toes. Thank God she'd fixed her hair and makeup. A friend of her father's? No way. This tall and lean guy was nowhere near her dad's age and had muscles that were evident underneath his gray t-shirt. Tattoos peeked out from under the sleeves and twisted down his arms to his wrists. Shaggy black hair framed a face with a square jaw and full lips.

Anatomy that she'd tried to forget about roared to life.

Which was ridiculous because the last thing she had time for was a man, even one as gorgeous as this one. She recognized him from high school, although they'd never been in the same circles since he'd been more of a bad boy.

Catching herself, she held out a hand and said coolly, "Hi, I'm Victoria. Wes's daughter."

His eyebrows rose over ice blue eyes. "I'm Nick."

She ignored the interest on his face as his lips quirked.

"Hey, Nick. Thanks for meeting us. Want to take a look around?" Wes shook his hand.

"Sure." Nick pulled a small notebook from his back pocket and a pencil from behind his ear. "What are you looking to do to the place?"

Victoria tried to bring her thoughts back to the business. Her dad was up to something, she could tell. He would've never hired out the job to someone else, even if he was retired, because he'd want to do it for her.

Wes glanced at her. "Ask her. She's the designer." His phone rang. "It's your mother. I'll take this outside."

Victoria watched him leave with a mutinous glare.

"So, Victoria. What do you want to do with the space?" His voice hinted at his amusement.

"You think this is funny?" She pursed her lips. "They're trying to set us up. It's mortifying." How could Nick not see what was going on? He definitely looked like the type who could get his own dates. If her sisters knew about this she was going to rain hell down on them.

Nick shrugged, the muscles in his torso and shoulders catching her eye. "I think it's funny. Wes told me he had a client for me. Didn't say it was one of his beautiful daughters."

Heat unfurled in her abdomen. She told her brain to tell her newly awakened anatomy to slow its role. "Where do we go from here?"

"I hear there's a new restaurant on the boardwalk we could try out." At her glare, he laughed.

The laugh shot straight to her core.

"I could design you an awesome office space. I am good at what I do. We can ignore the fact that our parents are working against us. Or we can make them happy and go out. I do love my mother very much, and this would make her very happy."

She couldn't help but smile. He was a charmer. "How about you design my awesome office space and we ignore our parents?"

"Sure, we can do that. But you can't blame a man for trying." Nick turned to the room. "So, the space?"

"Well, first of all I want that hideous receptionist counter gone. Demolish it. I need an office of my own in the back, and a small break room with room for counter space, a table, and a fridge. I'm going to design it like a regular kitchen, without the oven. I'll need a unisex bathroom." She continued with details while he took notes.

"This shouldn't be hard to do. I'll have to start the designs and get your approval before going for the permit." He tucked the notebook back in his pocket, the pencil behind his ear.

"How long will the designs take?" She looked out toward the parking lot, past it toward the beach. Anywhere but at him. She couldn't let herself be tempted. A man was a complication she didn't need. Not with her daughters and her expanding business.

"A week, tops. I have a job I'm finishing now but it

shouldn't take too much of my time."

The door opened and her dad stepped back inside. "Your mother was having a small dinner crisis. Needs me to pick up some stuff on my way home."

"Does she now?" Victoria narrowed her eyes so that he'd know she knew exactly what he was trying to do. Her dad deftly avoided eye contact. "Anyway, we're done here so I'm going to head home." She handed Nick her business card and tried to ignore the laughter in his eyes as she left.

About the Author:

I'm a multitasking mom of four. When not writing/doing laundry/changing diapers, I like to catch up on episodes of Supernatural and Castle. If you can't find me in front of the computer, I'm most likely watching my DVR.

I've been writing since the first grade, where I wrote a one page story titled "If I was an Indian". My warrior husband was going to be the best hunter, I was going to live in the best teepee and apparently, I was having an affair with the Chief. Racy, I know.

Of the things I'm addicted to sweet tea, movies, and books top the list. My favorite authors include Nora Roberts, Lauren Kate, Kresley Cole, and Gena Showalter. Few of many I love.

Thanks so much for reading!

Sam :)

Made in the USA
Charleston, SC
09 May 2015